PENGUIN BOOKS

PSMITH JOURNALIS[T]

P. G. Wodehouse was born in Guildford, England, in 1881 and educated at Dulwich College. After working for the Hong Kong and Shanghai Bank for two years, he left to earn his living as a journalist and storywriter, writing the 'By the Way' column in the old London *Globe*. He also contributed a series of school stories to a magazine for boys, *The Captain*, in one of which Psmith made his first appearance. Wodehouse visited the United States in 1904 and again in 1909, when he sold two short stories to *Cosmopolitan* and *Collier's* and decided to remain in America. In 1914 he sold a serial to *The Saturday Evening Post*, and for the next twenty-five years almost all his books appeared first in this magazine. With Jerome Kern, whom he had met in England, and Guy Bolton, Wodehouse worked on musicals for the Princess Theater starting in 1915. He subsequently wrote some sixteen plays, both by himself and with Bolton, and the lyrics of eighteen musical comedies with such composers as Victor Herbert, George Gershwin, Sigmund Romberg, and Rudolf Friml. Wodehouse married in 1914 and became a United States citizen in 1956. He wrote over ninety books, and his work has won worldwide acclaim, being translated into many languages. The London *Times* hailed him as 'a comic genius recognized in his lifetime as a classic and an old master of farce.' P. G. Wodehouse said: 'I believe there are two ways of writing novels. One is mine, making a sort of musical comedy without music and ignoring real life altogether; the other is going right deep down into life and not caring a damn.' He was created a Knight of the British Empire in the New Year's Honours List in 1975. In a B.B.C. interview he said that he had no ambitions left now that he had been knighted and there was a waxwork of him in Madame Tussard's. He died on St. Valentine's Day in 1975 at the age of ninety-three.

P. G. Wodehouse

Psmith Journalist

Penguin Books

Penguin Books Ltd, Harmondsworth,
Middlesex, England
Penguin Books, 40 West 23rd Street,
New York, New York 10010, U.S.A.
Penguin Books Australia Ltd, Ringwood,
Victoria, Australia
Penguin Books Canada Limited, 2801 John Street,
Markham, Ontario, Canada L3R 1B4
Penguin Books (N.Z.) Ltd, 182–190 Wairau Road,
Auckland 10, New Zealand

First published 1915
Published in Penguin Books 1970
Reprinted 1971, 1975, 1979, 1981, 1982, 1983

Printed in the United States of America by
George Banta Co., Inc., Harrisonburg, Virginia
Set in Intertype Times

Contents

Preface 7
1. 'Cosy Moments' 9
2. Billy Windsor 13
3. At 'The Gardenia' 17
4. Bat Jarvis 23
5. Planning Improvements 29
6. The Tenements 34
7. Visitors at the Office 38
8. The Honeyed Word 41
9. Full Steam Ahead 47
10. Going Some 51
11. The Man at the Astor 60
12. A Red Taximeter 67
13. Reviewing the Situation 71
14. The Highfield 76
15. An Addition to the Staff 84
16. The First Battle 89
17. Guerilla Warfare 98
18. An Episode by the Way 103
19. In Pleasant Street 108
20. Cornered 113
21. The Battle of Pleasant Street 121
22. Concerning Mr Waring 129
23. Reductions in the Staff 134
24. A Gathering of Cat-Specialists 142
25. Trapped 150
26. A Friend in Need 159
27. Psmith Concludes His Ride 164
28. Standing Room Only 170
29. The Knock-out for Mr Waring 178
30. Conclusion 185

Preface

The conditions of life in New York are so different from those of London that a story of this kind calls for a little explanation. There are several million inhabitants of New York. Not all of them eke out a precarious livelihood by murdering one another, but there is a definite section of the population which murders – not casually, on the spur of the moment, but on definitely commercial lines at so many dollars per murder. The 'gangs' of New York exist in fact. I have not invented them. Most of the incidents in this story are based on actual happenings. The Rosenthal case, where four men, headed by a genial individual calling himself 'Gyp the Blood' shot a fellow-citizen in cold blood in a spot as public and fashionable as Piccadilly Circus and escaped in a motor-car, made such a stir a few years ago that the noise of it was heard all over the world and not, as is generally the case with the doings of the gangs, in New York only. Rosenthal caes on a smaller and less sensational scale are frequent occurrences on Manhatten Island. It was the prominence of the victim rather than the unusual nature of the occurrence that excited the New York press. Most gang victims get a quarter of a column in small type.

New York, 1915   P. G. WODEHOUSE

1. 'Cosy Moments'

The man in the street would not have known it, but a great crisis was imminent in New York journalism.

Everything seemed much as usual in the city. The cars ran blithely on Broadway. Newsboys shouted 'Wux-try!' into the ears of nervous pedestrians with their usual Caruso-like vim. Society passed up and down Fifth Avenue in its automobiles, and was there a furrow of anxiety upon Society's brow? – None. At a thousand street corners a thousand policemen preserved their air of massive superiority to the things of this world. Not one of them showed the least sign of perturbation. Nevertheless, the crisis was at hand. Mr J. Fillken Wilberfloss, editor-in-chief of *Cosy Moments,* was about to leave his post and start on a ten weeks' holiday.

In New York one may find every class of paper which the imagination can conceive. Every grade of society is catered for. If an Esquimau came to New York, the first thing he would find on the book-stalls in all probability would be the *Blubber Magazine,* or some similar production written by Esquimaux for Esquimaux. Everybody reads in New York, and reads all the time. The New Yorker peruses his favourite paper while he is being jammed into a crowded compartment on the subway or leaping like an antelope into a moving street car.

There was thus a public for *Cosy Moments. Cosy Moments,* as its name (an inspiration of Mr Wilberfloss's own) is designed to imply, is a journal for the home. It is the sort of paper which the father of the family is expected to take home with him from his office and read aloud to the chicks before bed-time. It was founded by its proprietor, Mr Benjamin White, as an antidote to yellow journalism. One is forced to admit that up to the present yellow journalism seems to be competing against it with a certain measure of success. Headlines are still of as generous a size as heretofore, and there is no tendency on the part of editors to scamp the details of the last murder-case.

Nevertheless, *Cosy Moments* thrives. It has its public.

Its contents are mildly interesting, if you like that sort of thing. There is a 'Moments in the Nursery' page, conducted by Luella Granville Waterman, to which parents are invited to contribute the bright speeches of their offspring, and which bristles with little stories about the nursery canary, by Jane (aged six), and other works of rising young authors. There is a 'Moments of Meditation' page, conducted by the Reverend Edwin T. Philpotts; a 'Moments Among the Masters' page, consisting of assorted chunks looted from the literature of the past, when foreheads were bulgy and thoughts profound, by Mr Wilberfloss himself; one or two other pages; a short story; answers to correspondents on domestic matters; and a 'Moments of Mirth' page, conducted by an alleged humorist of the name of B. Henderson Asher, which is about the most painful production ever served up to a confiding public.

The guiding spirit of *Cosy Moments* was Mr Wilberfloss. Circumstances had left the development of the paper mainly to him. For the past twelve months the proprietor had been away in Europe, taking the waters at Carlsbad, and the sole control of *Cosy Moments* had passed into the hands of Mr Wilberfloss. Nor had he proved unworthy of the trust or unequal to the duties. In that year *Cosy Moments* had reached the highest possible level of domesticity. Anything not calculated to appeal to the home had been rigidly excluded. And as a result the circulation had increased steadily. Two extra pages had been added, 'Moments Among the Shoppers' and 'Moments with Society'. And the advertisements had grown in volume. But the work had told upon the Editor. Work of that sort carries its penalties with it. Success means absorption, and absorption spells softening of the brain. Whether it was the strain of digging into the literature of the past every week, or the effort of reading B. Henderson Asher's 'Moments of Mirth' is uncertain. At any rate, his duties, combined with the heat of a New York summer, had sapped Mr Wilberfloss's health to such an extent that the doctor had ordered him ten weeks' complete rest in the mountains. This Mr Wilberfloss could, perhaps, have endured, if this had been all. There are worse places than the mountains of America in which to spend ten weeks of the tail-end of summer, when the sun has ceased to grill and the mosquitoes have relaxed their exertions. But it was not all. The doctor, a far-seeing man who went down to first causes, had absolutely declined to consent to Mr Wilberfloss's suggestion that he should keep in touch with the paper during his vacation. He was adamant. He had seen copies of *Cosy Moments* once or twice, and he refused to permit a man in the editor's state of health to come in contact with Luella Granville Waterman's 'Moments in the Nursery' and B. Henderson Asher's 'Moments of Mirth'. The medicine-man put his foot down firmly.

'You must not see so much as the cover of the paper for ten weeks,' he said. 'And I'm not so sure that it shouldn't be longer. You must forget that such a paper exists. You must dismiss the whole thing from your mind, live in the open, and develop a little flesh and muscle.'

To Mr Wilberfloss the sentence was almost equivalent to penal servitude. It was with tears in his voice that he was giving his final instructions to his sub-editor, in whose charge the paper would be left during his absence. He had taken a long time doing this. For two days he had been fussing in and out of the office, to the discontent of its inmates, more especially Billy Windsor, the sub-editor, who was now listening moodily to the last harangue of the series, with the air of one whose heart is not in the subject. Billy Windsor was a tall, wiry, loose-jointed young man, with unkempt hair and the general demeanour of a caged eagle. Looking at him, one could picture him astride of a broncho, rounding up cattle, or cooking his dinner at a camp-fire. Somehow he did not seem to fit into the *Cosy Moments* atmosphere.

'Well, I think that that is all, Mr Windsor,' chirruped the editor. He was a little man with a long neck and large *pince-nez,* and he always chirruped. 'You understand the general lines on which I think the paper should be conducted?' The sub-editor nodded. Mr Wilberfloss made him tired. Sometimes he made him more tired than at other times. At the present moment he filled him with an aching weariness. The editor meant well, and was full of zeal, but he had a habit of covering and re-covering the ground. He possessed the art of saying the same obvious thing in a number of different ways to a degree which is found usually only in politicians. If Mr Wilberfloss had been a politician, he would have been one of those dealers in glittering generalities who used to be fashionable in American politics.

'There is just one thing,' he continued. 'Mrs Julia Burdett Parslow is a little inclined – I may have mentioned this before –'

'You did,' said the sub-editor.

Mr Wilberfloss chirruped on, unchecked.

'A little inclined to be late with her "Moments with Budding Girlhood". If this should happen while I am away, just write her a letter, quite a pleasant letter, you understand, pointing out the necessity of being in good time. The machinery of a weekly paper, of course, cannot run smoothly unless contributors are in good time with their copy. She is a very sensible woman, and she will understand, I am sure, if you point it out to her.'

The sub-editor nodded.

'And there is just one other thing. I wish you would correct a slight tendency I have noticed lately in Mr Asher to be just a trifle – well, not precisely *risky*, but perhaps a shade *broad* in his humour.'

'His what?' said Billy Windsor.

'Mr Asher is a very sensible man, and he will be the first to acknowledge that his sense of humour has led him just a little beyond the bounds. You understand? Well, that is all, I think. Now I must really be going, or I shall miss my train. Good-bye, Mr Windsor.'

'Good-bye,' said the sub-editor thankfully.

At the door Mr Wilberfloss paused with the air of an exile bidding farewell to his native land, sighed, and trotted out.

Billy Windsor put his feet upon the table, and with a deep scowl resumed his task of reading the proofs of Luella Granville Waterman's 'Moments in the Nursery'.

2. Billy Windsor

Billy Windsor had started life twenty-five years before this story opens on his father's ranch in Wyoming. From there he had gone to a local paper of the type whose Society column consists of such items as 'Pawnee Jim Williams was to town yesterday with a bunch of other cheap skates. We take this opportunity of once more informing Jim that he is a liar and a skunk,' and whose editor works with a revolver on his desk and another in his hip-pocket. Graduating from this, he had proceeded to a reporter's post on a daily paper in a Kentucky town, where there were blood feuds and other Southern devices for preventing life from becoming dull. All this time New York, the magnet, had been tugging at him. All reporters dream of reaching New York. At last, after four years on the Kentucky paper, he had come East, minus the lobe of one ear and plus a long scar that ran diagonally across his left shoulder, and had worked without much success as a free-lance. He was tough and ready for anything that might come his way, but these things are a great deal a matter of luck. The cub-reporter cannot make a name for himself unless he is favoured by fortune. Things had not come Billy Windsor's way. His work had been confined to turning in reports of fires and small street-accidents, which the various papers to which he supplied them cut down to a couple of inches.

Billy had been in a bad way when he had happened upon the sub-editorship of *Cosy Moments*. He despised the work with all his heart, and the salary was infinitesimal. But it was regular, and for a while Billy felt that a regular salary was the greatest thing on earth. But he still dreamed of winning through to a post on one of the big New York dailies, where there was something doing and a man would have a chance of showing what was in him.

The unfortunate thing, however, was that *Cosy Moments* took up his time so completely. He had no chance of attracting the notice of big editors by his present work, and he had no leisure for doing any other.

All of which may go to explain why his normal aspect was that of a caged eagle.

To him, brooding over the outpourings of Luella Granville Waterman, there entered Pugsy Maloney, the office-boy, bearing a struggling cat.

'Say!' said Pugsy.

He was a nonchalant youth, with a freckled, mask-like face, the expression of which never varied. He appeared unconscious of the cat. Its existence did not seem to occur to him.

'Well?' said Billy, looking up. 'Hello, what have you got there?'

Master Maloney eyed the cat, as if he were seeing it for the first time.

'It's a kitty what I got in de street,' he said.

'Don't hurt the poor brute. Put her down.'

Master Maloney obediently dropped the cat, which sprang nimbly on to an upper shelf of the book-case.

'I wasn't hoitin' her,' he said, without emotion. 'Dere was two fellers in de street sickin' a dawg on to her. An' I come up an' says, "G'wan! What do youse t'ink you're doin', fussin' de poor dumb animal?" An' one of de guys, he says, "G'wan! Who do youse t'ink youse is?" An' I says, "I'm de guy what's goin' to swat youse one on de coco if youse don't quit fussin' de poor dumb animal." So wit dat he makes a break at swattin' me one, but I swats him one, an' I swats de odder feller one, an' den I swats dem bote some more, an' I gets de kitty, an' I brings her in here, cos I t'inks maybe youse'll look after her.'

And having finished this Homeric narrative, Master Maloney fixed an expressionless eye on the ceiling, and was silent.

Billy Windsor, like most men of the plains, combined the toughest of muscle with the softest of hearts. He was always ready at any moment to become the champion of the oppressed on the slightest provocation. His alliance with Pugsy Maloney had begun on the occasion when he had rescued that youth from the clutches of a large Negro, who, probably from the soundest of motives, was endeavouring to slay him. Billy had not inquired into the rights and wrongs of the matter: he had merely sailed in and rescued the office-boy. And Pugsy, though he had made no verbal comment on the affair, had shown in many ways that he was not ungrateful.

'Bully for you, Pugsy!' he cried. 'You're a little sport. Here' — he produced a dollar-bill — 'go out and get some milk for the poor brute. She's probably starving. Keep the change.'

'Sure thing,' assented Master Maloney. He strolled slowly out, while Billy Windsor, mounting a chair, proceeded to chirrup and snap his fingers in the effort to establish the foundations of an *entente cordiale* with the rescued cat.

By the time that Pugsy had returned, carrying a five-cent bottle of milk, the animal had vacated the book-shelf, and was sitting on the table, washing her face. The milk having been poured into the lid of a tobacco-tin, in lieu of a saucer, she suspended her operations and adjourned for refreshments Billy, business being business, turned again to Luella Granville Waterman, but Pugsy, having no immediate duties on hand, concentrated himself on the cat.

'Say!' he said.

'Well?'

'Dat kitty.'

'What about her?'

'Pipe de leather collar she's wearing.'

Billy had noticed earlier in the proceedings that a narrow leather collar encircled the cat's neck. He had not paid any particular attention to it. 'What about it?' he said.

'Guess I know where dat kitty belongs. Dey all have dose collars. I guess she's one of Bat Jarvis's kitties. He's got a lot of dem for fair, and every one wit one of dem collars round deir neck.'

'Who's Bat Jarvis? Do you mean the gang-leader?'

'Sure. He's a cousin of mine,' said Master Maloney with pride.

'Is he?' said Billy. 'Nice sort of fellow to have in the family. So you think that's his cat?'

'Sure. He's got twenty-t'ree of dem, and dey all has dose collars.'

'Are you on speaking terms with the gentleman?'

'Huh?'

'Do you know Bat Jarvis to speak to?'

'Sure. He's me cousin.'

'Well, tell him I've got the cat, and that if he wants it he'd better come round to my place. You know where I live?'

'Sure.'

'Fancy you being a cousin of Bat's, Pugsy. Why did you never tell us? Are you going to join the gang some day?'

'Nope. Nothin' doin'. I'm goin' to be a cowboy.'

'Good for you. Well, you tell him when you see him. And now, my lad, out you get, because if I'm interrupted any more I shan't get through tonight.'

'Sure,' said Master Maloney, retiring.

'Oh, and Pugsy ..'

'Huh?'

'Go out and get a good big basket. I shall want one to carry this animal home in.'

'Sure,' said Master Maloney.

3. At 'The Gardenia'

'It would ill beseem me, Comrade Jackson,' said Psmith, thoughtfully sipping his coffee, 'to run down the metropolis of a great and friendly nation, but candour compels me to state that New York is in some respects a singularly blighted town.'

'What's the matter with it?' asked Mike.

'Too decorous, Comrade Jackson. I came over here principally, it is true, to be at your side, should you be in any way persecuted by scoundrels. But at the same time I confess that at the back of my mind there lurked a hope that stirring adventures might come my way. I had heard so much of the place. Report had it that an earnest seeker after amusement might have a tolerably spacious rag in this modern Byzantium. I thought that a few weeks here might restore that keen edge to my nervous system which the languor of the past term had in a measure blunted. I wished my visit to be a tonic rather than a sedative. I anticipated that on my return the cry would go round Cambridge, "Psmith has been to New York. He is full of oats. For he on honey-dew hath fed, and drunk the milk of Paradise. He is hot stuff. Rah!" But what do we find?'

He paused, and lit a cigarette.

'What do we find?' he asked again.

'I don't know,' said Mike. 'What?'

'A very judicious query, Comrade Jackson. What, indeed? We find a town very like London. A quiet, self-respecting town, admirable to the apostle of social reform, but disappointing to one who, like myself, arrives with a brush and a little bucket of red paint, all eager for a treat. I have been here a week, and I have not seen a single citizen clubbed by a policeman. No Negroes dance cake-walks in the street. No cowboy has let off his revolver at random in Broadway. The cables flash the message across the ocean, "Psmith is losing his illusions".'

Mike had come to America with a team of the M.C.C. which was touring the cricket-playing section of the United States. Psmith had accompanied him in a private capacity. It was the end of their first year at Cambridge, and Mike, with a century against Oxford to his credit, had been one of the first to be invited to join the tour. Psmith, who had played cricket in a rather desultory way at the University, had not risen to these heights. He had merely taken the opportunity of Mike's visit to the other side to accompany him. Cambridge had proved pleasant to Psmith, but a trifle quiet. He had welcomed the chance of getting a change of scene.

So far the visit had failed to satisfy him. Mike, whose tastes in pleasure were simple, was delighted with everything. The cricket so far had been rather of the picnic order, but it was very pleasant; and there was no limit to the hospitality with which the visitors were treated. It was this more than anything which had caused Psmith's grave disapproval of things American. He was not a member of the team, so that the advantages of the hospitality did not reach him. He had all the disadvantages. He saw far too little of Mike. When he wished to consult his confidential secretary and adviser on some aspect of Life, that invaluable official was generally absent at dinner with the rest of the team. Tonight was one of the rare occasions when Mike could get away. Psmith was becoming bored. New York is a better city than London to be alone in, but it is never pleasant to be alone in any big city.

As they sat discussing New York's shortcomings over their coffee, a young man passed them, carrying a basket, and seated himself at the next table. He was a tall, loose-jointed young man, with unkempt hair.

A waiter made an ingratiating gesture towards the basket, but the young man stopped him. 'Not on your life, sonny,' he said. 'This stays right here.' He placed it carefully on the floor beside his chair, and proceeded to order dinner.

Psmith watched him thoughtfully.

'I have a suspicion, Comrade Jackson,' he said, 'that this will prove to be a somewhat stout fellow. If possible, we will engage him in conversation. I wonder what he's got in the basket. I must get my Sherlock Holmes system to work. What is the most likely thing for a man to have in a basket? You would reply, in your unthinking way, "sandwiches". Error. A man with a basketful of sandwiches does not need to dine at restaurants. We must try again.'

The young man at the next table had ordered a jug of milk to be accompanied by a saucer. These having arrived, he proceeded to lift the basket on to his lap, pour the milk into the saucer, and remove the lid from the basket. Instantly, with a yell which made the young man's table the centre of interest to all the diners, a large grey cat shot up like a rocket, and darted across the room. Psmith watched with silent interest.

It is hard to astonish the waiters at a New York restaurant, but when the cat performed this feat there was a squeal of surprise all round the room. Waiters rushed to and fro, futile but energetic. The cat, having secured a strong strategic position on the top of a large oil-painting which hung on the far wall, was expressing loud disapproval of the efforts of one of the waiters to drive it from its post with a walking-stick. The young man, seeing these manoeuvres, uttered a wrathful shout, and rushed to the rescue.

'Comrade Jackson,' said Psmith, rising, 'we must be in this.'

When they arrived on the scene of hostilities, the young man had just possessed himself of the walking-stick, and was deep in a complex argument with the head-waiter on the ethics of the matter. The head-waiter, a stout impassive German, had taken his stand on a point of etiquette. 'Id is,' he said, 'to bring gats into der grill-room vorbidden. No gendleman would gats into der grill-room bring. Der gendleman – '

The young man meanwhile was making enticing sounds, to which the cat was maintaining an attitude of reserved hostility. He turned furiously on the head-waiter.

'For goodness' sake,' he cried, 'can't you see the poor brute's scared stiff? Why don't you clear your gang of German comedians away, and give her a chance to come down?'

'Der gendleman – ' argued the head-waiter.

Psmith stepped forward and touched him on the arm.

'May I have a word with you in private?'

'Zo?'

Psmith drew him away.

'You don't know who that is?' he whispered, nodding towards the young man.

'No gendleman he is,' asserted the head-waiter. 'Der gendleman would not der gat into – '

Psmith shook his head pityingly.

'These petty matters of etiquette are not for his Grace – but, hush, he wishes to preserve his incognito.'

'Incognito?'

'You understand. You are a man of the world, Comrade – may I call you Freddie? You understand, Comrade Freddie, that in a man in his Grace's position a few little eccentricities may be pardoned. You follow me, Frederick?'

The head-waiter's eye rested upon the young man with a new interest and respect.

'He is noble?' he inquired with awe.

'He is here strictly incognito, you understand,' said Psmith warningly. The head-waiter nodded.

The young man meanwhile had broken down the cat's reserve, and was now standing with her in his arms, apparently anxious to fight all-comers in her defence. The head-waiter approached deferentially.

'Der gendleman,' he said, indicating Psmith, who beamed in a friendly manner though his eye-glass, 'haf everything explained. All will now quite satisfactory be.'

The young man looked inquiringly at Psmith, who winked encouragingly. The head-waiter bowed.

'Let me present Comrade Jackson,' said Psmith, 'the pet of our English Smart Set. I am Psmith, one of the Shropshire Psmiths. This is a great moment. Shall we be moving back? We were about to order a second instalment of coffee, to correct the effects of a fatiguing day. Perhaps you would care to join us?'

'Sure,' said the alleged duke.

'This,' said Psmith, when they were seated, and the head-

waiter had ceased to hover, 'is a great meeting. I was com-
plaining with some acerbity to Comrade Jackson, before you
introduced your very interesting performing-animal speciality,
that things in New York were too quiet, too decorous. I have an
inkling, Comrade – '

'Windsor's my name.'

'I have an inkling, Comrade Windsor, that we see eye to eye
on the subject.'

'I guess that's right. I was raised in the plains, and I lived in
Kentucky a while. There's more doing there in a day than there
is here in a month. Say, how did you fix it with the old man?'

'With Comrade Freddie? I have a certain amount of
influence with him. He is content to order his movements in the
main by my judgement. I assured him that all would be well, and
he yielded.' Psmith gazed with interest at the cat, which was
lapping milk from the saucer. 'Are you training that animal for
a show of some kind, Comrade Windsor, or is it a domestic
pet?'

'I've adopted her. The office-boy on our paper got her away
from a dog this morning, and gave her to me.'

'Your paper?'

'*Cosy Moments*,' said Billy Windsor, with a touch of
shame.

'*Cosy Moments*?' said Psmith reflectively. 'I regret that the
bright little sheet has not come my way up to the present. I must
seize an early opportunity of perusing it.'

'Don't you do it.'

'You've no parental pride in the little journal?'

'It's bad enough to hurt,' said Billy Windsor disgustedly. 'If
you really want to see it, come along with me to my place, and
I'll show you a copy.'

'It will be a pleasure,' said Psmith. 'Comrade Jackson, have
you any previous engagement for tonight?'

'I'm not doing anything,' said Mike.

'Then let us stagger forth with Comrade Windsor. While he is
loading up that basket, we will be collecting our hats. . . . I am
not half sure, Comrade Jackson,' he added, as they walked out,
'that Comrade Windsor may not prove to be the genial spirit

for whom I have been searching. If you could give me your undivided company, I should ask no more. But with you constantly away, mingling with the gay throng, it is imperative that I have some solid man to accompany me in my ramblings hither and thither. It is possible that Comrade Windsor may possess the qualifications necessary for the post. But here he comes. Let us foregather with him and observe him in private life before arriving at any premature decision.'

4. Bat Jarvis

Billy Windsor lived in a single room on East Fourteenth Street. Space in New York is valuable, and the average bachelor's apartments consist of one room with a bathroom opening off it. During the daytime this one room loses all traces of being used for sleeping purposes at night. Billy Windsor's room was very much like a public-school study. Along one wall ran a settee. At night this became a bed; but in the daytime it was a settee and nothing but a settee. There was no space for a great deal of furniture. There was one rocking-chair, two ordinary chairs, a table, a book-stand, a typewriter – nobody uses pens in New York – and on the walls a mixed collection of photographs, drawings, knives, and skins, relics of their owner's prairie days. Over the door was the head of a young bear.

Billy's first act on arriving in this sanctum was to release the cat, which, having moved restlessly about for some moments, finally came to the conclusion that there was no means of getting out, and settled itself on a corner of the settee. Psmith, sinking gracefully down beside it, stretched out his legs and lit a cigarette. Mike took one of the ordinary chairs; and Billy Windsor, planting himself in the rocker, began to rock rhythmically to and fro, a performance which he kept up untiringly all the time.

'A peaceful scene,' observed Psmith. 'Three great minds, keen, alert, restless during business hours, relax. All is calm and pleasant chit-chat. You have snug quarters up here, Comrade Windsor. I hold that there is nothing like one's own roof-tree. It is a great treat to one who, like myself, is located in one of these vast caravanserai – to be exact, the Astor – to pass a few moments in the quiet privacy of an apartment such as this.'

'It's beastly expensive at the Astor,' said Mike.

23

'The place has that drawback also. Anon, Comrade Jackson, I think we will hunt around for some such cubby-hole as this, built for two. Our nervous systems must be conserved.'

'On Fourth Avenue,' said Billy Windsor, 'you can get quite good flats very cheap. Furnished, too. You should move there. It's not much of a neighbourhood. I don't know if you mind that?'

'Far from it, Comrade Windsor. It is my aim to see New York in all its phases. If a certain amount of harmless revelry can be whacked out of Fourth Avenue, we must dash there with the vim of highly-trained smell-dogs. Are you with me, Comrade Jackson?'

'All right,' said Mike.

'And now, Comrade Windsor, it would be a pleasure to me to peruse that little journal of which you spoke. I have had so few opportunities of getting into touch with the literature of this great country.'

Billy Windsor stretched out an arm and pulled a bundle of papers from the book-stand. He tossed them on to the settee by Psmith's side.

'There you are,' he said, 'if you really feel like it. Don't say I didn't warn you. If you've got the nerve, read on.'

Psmith had picked up one of the papers when there came a shuffling of feet in the passage outside, followed by a knock upon the door. The next moment there appeared in the door-way a short, stout young man. There was an indescribable air of toughness about him partly due to the fact that he wore his hair in a well-oiled fringe almost down to his eyebrows, which gave him the appearance of having no forehead at all. His eyes were small and set close together. His mouth was wide; his jaw prominent. Not, in short, the sort of man you would have picked out on sight as a model citizen.

His entrance was marked by a curious sibilant sound, which, on acquaintance, proved to be a whistled tune. During the interview which followed, except when he was speaking, the visitor whistled softly and unceasingly.

'Mr Windsor?' he said to the company at large.

Psmith waved a hand towards the rocking-chair. 'That,' he

said, 'is Comrade Windsor. To your right is Comrade Jackson, England's favourite son. I am Psmith.'

The visitor blinked furtively, and whistled another tune. As he looked round the room, his eye fell on the cat. His face lit up.

'Say!' he said, stepping forward, and touching the cat's collar, 'mine, mister.'

'Are you Bat Jarvis?' asked Windsor with interest.

'Sure,' said the visitor, not without a touch of complacency, as of a monarch abandoning his incognito.

For Mr Jarvis was a celebrity.

By profession he was a dealer in animals, birds and snakes. He had a fancier's shop in Groome Street, in the heart of the Bowery. This was on the ground-floor. His living abode was in the upper storey of that house, and it was there that he kept the twenty-three cats whose necks were adorned with leather collars, and whose numbers had so recently been reduced to twenty-two. But it was not the fact that he possessed twenty-three cats with leather collars that made Mr Jarvis a celebrity. A man may win a purely local reputation, if only for eccentricity, by such means. But Mr Jarvis's reputation was far from being purely local. Broadway knew him, and the Tenderloin. Tammany Hall knew him. Long Island City knew him. In the underworld of New York his name was a byword. For Bat Jarvis was the leader of the famous Groome Street Gang, the most noted of all New York's collections of Apaches. More, he was the founder and originator of it. And, curiously enough, it had come into being from motives of sheer benevolence. In Groome Street in those days there had been a dance-hall, named the Shamrock and presided over by one Maginnis, an Irishman and a friend of Bat's. At the Shamrock nightly dances were given and well attended by the youth of the neighbourhood at ten cents a head. All might have been well, had it not been for certain other youths of the neighbourhood who did not dance and so had to seek other means of getting rid of their surplus energy. It was the practice of these light-hearted sportsmen to pay their ten cents for admittance, and once in, to make hay. And this habit, Mr Maginnis found, was having a marked effect on his earnings. For genuine lovers of the dance fought shy of a place where at any moment Philistines might burst in and break heads and furniture. In this crisis the proprietor thought of his friend Bat Jarvis. Bat at that time had a solid reputation as a man of his hands. It is true that, as his detractors pointed out, he had killed no one – a defect which he had subsequently corrected; but his admirers based his claim to respect on his many meritorious performances with fists and with the black-jack. And Mr Maginnis for one held him in the very highest esteem. To Bat accordingly he went, and laid his painful case before him. He offered him a handsome salary to be on hand at the nightly dances and check undue revelry by his own robust methods. Bat had accepted the offer. He had gone to Shamrock Hall; and with him, faithful adherents, had gone such stalwarts as Long Otto, Red Logan, Tommy Jefferson, and Pete Brodie. Shamrock Hall became a place of joy and order; and – more important still – the nucleus of the Groome Street Gang had been formed. The work progressed. Off-shoots of the main gang sprang up here and there about the East Side. Small thieves, pickpockets and the like, flocked to Mr Jarvis as their tribal leader and protector and he protected them. For he, with his followers, were of use to the politicians. The New York gangs, and especially the Groome Street Gang, have brought to a fine art the gentle practice of 'repeating'; which, broadly speaking, is the art of voting a number of different times at different polling-stations on election days. A man who can vote, say, ten times in a single day for you, and who controls a great number of followers who are also prepared, if they like you, to vote ten times in a single day for you, is worth cultivating. So the politicians passed the word to the police, and the police left the Groome Street Gang unmolested and they waxed fat and flourished.

Such was Bat Jarvis.

'Pipe de collar,' said Mr Jarvis, touching the cat's neck. 'Mine, mister.'

'Pugsy said it must be,' said Billy Windsor. 'We found two fellows setting a dog on to it, so we took it in for safety.'

Mr Jarvis nodded approval

'There's a basket here, if you want it,' said Billy

'Nope. Here, kit.'

Mr Jarvis stooped, and, still whistling softly, lifted the cat. He looked round the company, met Psmith's eye-glass, was transfixed by it for a moment, and finally turned again to Billy Windsor.

'Say!' he said, and paused. 'Obliged,' he added.

He shifted the cat on to his left arm, and extended his right hand to Billy.

'Shake!' he said.

Billy did so.

Mr Jarvis continued to stand and whistle for a few moments more.

'Say!' he said at length, fixing his roving gaze once more upon Billy. 'Obliged. Fond of de kit, I am.'

Psmith nodded approvingly.

'And rightly', he said. 'Rightly, Comrade Jarvis. She is not unworthy of your affection. A most companionable animal, full of the highest spirits. Her knockabout act in the restaurant would have satisfied the most jaded critic. No diner-out can afford to be without such a cat. Such a cat spells death to boredom.'

Mr Jarvis eyed him fixedly, as if pondering over his remarks. Then he turned to Billy again.

'Say!' he said. 'Any time you're in bad. Glad to be of service. You know the address. Groome Street. Bat Jarvis. Good night. Obliged.'

He paused and whistled a few more bars, then nodded to Psmith and Mike, and left the room. They heard him shuffling downstairs.

'A blithe spirit,' said Psmith. 'Not garrulous, perhaps, but what of that? I am a man of few words myself. Comrade Jarvis's massive silences appeal to me. He seems to have taken a fancy to you, Comrade Windsor.'

Billy Windsor laughed.

'I don't know that he's just the sort of side-partner I'd go out of my way to choose, from what I've heard about him.

Still, if one got mixed up with any of that East-Side crowd, he would be a mighty useful friend to have. I guess there's no harm done by getting him grateful.'

'Assuredly not,' said Psmith. 'We should not despise the humblest. And now, Comrade Windsor,' he said, taking up the paper again, 'let me concentrate myself tensely on this very entertaining little journal of yours. Comrade Jackson, here is one for you. For sound, clear-headed criticism,' he added to Billy, 'Comrade Jackson's name is a by-word in our English literary *salons*. His opinion will be both of interest and of profit to you, Comrade Windsor.'

5. Planning Improvements

'By the way,' said Psmith, 'what is your exact position on this paper? Practically, we know well, you are its back-bone, its life-blood; but what is your technical position? When your proprietor is congratulating himself on having secured the ideal man for your job, what precise job does he congratulate himself on having secured the ideal man for?'

'I'm sub-editor.'

'Merely sub? You deserve a more responsible post than that, Comrade Windsor. Where is your proprietor? I must button-hole him and point out to him what a wealth of talent he is allowing to waste itself. You must have scope.'

'He's in Europe. At Carlsbad, or somewhere. He never comes near the paper. He just sits tight and draws the profits. He lets the editor look after things. Just at present I'm acting as editor.'

'Ah! then at last you have your big chance. You are free, untrammelled.'

'You bet I'm not,' said Billy Windsor. 'Guess again. There's no room for developing free untrammelled ideas on this paper. When you've looked at it, you'll see that each page is run by some one. I'm simply the fellow who minds the shop.'

Psmith clicked his tongue sympathetically. 'It is like setting a gifted French chef to wash up dishes,' he said. 'A man of your undoubted powers, Comrade Windsor, should have more scope. That is the cry, more scope. I must look into this matter. When I gaze at your broad, bulging forehead, when I see the clear light of intelligence in your eyes, and hear the grey matter splashing restlessly about in your cerebellum, I say to myself without hesitation, "Comrade Windsor must have more scope." ' He looked at Mike, who was turning over the leaves of his copy of *Cosy Moments* in a sort of dull despair. 'Well, Comrade Jackson, and what is your verdict?'

Mike looked at Billy Windsor. He wished to be polite, yet he could find nothing polite to say. Billy interpreted the look.

'Go on,' he said. 'Say it. It can't be worse than what I think.'

'I expect some people would like it awfully,' said Mike.

'They must, or they wouldn't buy it. I've never met any of them yet, though.'

Psmith was deep in Luella Granville Waterman's 'Moments in the Nursery'. He turned to Billy Windsor.

'Luella Granville Waterman,' he said, 'is not by any chance your *nom-de-plume,* Comrade Windsor?'

'Not on your life. Don't think it.'

'I am glad,' said Psmith courteously. 'For, speaking as man to man, I must confess that for sheer, concentrated bilge she gets away with the biscuit with almost insolent ease. Luella Granville Waterman must go.'

'How do you mean?'

'She must go,' repeated Psmith firmly. 'Your first act, now that you have swiped the editorial chair, must be to sack her.'

'But, say, I can't. The editor thinks a heap of her stuff.'

'We cannot help his troubles. We must act for the good of the paper. Moreover, you said, I think, that he was away?'

'So he is. But he'll come back.'

'Sufficient unto the day, Comrade Windsor. I have a suspicion that he will be the first to approve your action. His holiday will have cleared his brain. Make a note of improvement number one – the sacking of Luella Granville Waterman.'

'I guess it'll be followed pretty quick by improvement number two – the sacking of William Windsor. I can't go monkeying about with the paper that way.'

Psmith reflected for a moment.

'Has this job of yours any special attractions for you, Comrade Windsor?'

'I guess not.'

'As I suspected. You yearn for scope. What exactly are your ambitions?'

'I want to get a job on one of the big dailies. I don't see how I'm going to fix it, though, at the present rate.'

Psmith rose, and tapped him earnestly on the chest.

'Comrade Windsor, you have touched the spot. You are wasting the golden hours of your youth. You must move. You must hustle. You must make Windsor of *Cosy Moments* a name to conjure with. You must boost this sheet up till New York rings with your exploits. On the present lines that is impossible. You must strike out a line for yourself. You must show the world that even *Cosy Moments* cannot keep a good man down.'

He resumed his seat.

'How do you mean?' said Billy Windsor.

Psmith turned to Mike.

'Comrade Jackson, if you were editing this paper, is there a single feature you would willingly retain?'

'I don't think there is,' said Mike. 'It's all pretty bad rot.'

'My opinion in a nutshell,' said Psmith, approvingly. 'Comrade Jackson,' he explained, turning to Billy, 'has a secure reputation on the other side for the keenness and lucidity of his views upon literature. You may safely build upon him. In England when Comrade Jackson says "Turn" we all turn. Now, my views on the matter are as follows. *Cosy Moments,* in my opinion (worthless, were it not backed by such a virtuoso as Comrade Jackson), needs more snap, more go. All these putrid pages must disappear. Letters must be dispatched tomorrow morning, informing Luella Granville Waterman and the others (and in particular B. Henderson Asher, who from a cursory glance strikes me as an ideal candidate for a lethal chamber) that, unless they cease their contributions instantly, you will be compelled to place yourself under police protection. After that we can begin to move.'

Billy Windsor sat and rocked himself in his chair without replying. He was trying to assimilate this idea. So far the grandeur of it had dazed him. It was too spacious, too revolutionary. Could it be done? It would undoubtedly mean the sack when Mr J. Fillken Wilberfloss returned and found the apple of his eye torn asunder and, so to speak, deprived of its choicest pips. On the other hand. .... His brow suddenly cleared. After all, what was the sack? One crowded hour of glorious life is worth an age without a name, and he would have no name as long as he clung to his present position. The editor would be away ten weeks. He would have ten weeks in which to try himself out. Hope leaped within him. In ten weeks he could change *Cosy Moments* into a real live paper. He wondered that the idea had not occurred to him before. The trifling fact that the despised journal was the property of Mr Benjamin White, and that he had no right whatever to tinker with it without that gentleman's approval, may have occurred to him, but, if it did, it occurred so momentarily that he did not notice it. In these crises one cannot think of everything.

'I'm on,' he said, briefly.

Psmith smiled approvingly.

'That,' he said, 'is the right spirit. You will, I fancy, have little cause to regret your decision. Fortunately, if I may say so, I happen to have a certain amount of leisure just now. It is at your disposal. I have had little experience of journalistic work, but I foresee that I shall be a quick learner. I will become your sub-editor, without salary.'

'Bully for you,' said Billy Windsor.

'Comrade Jackson,' continued Psmith, 'is unhappily more fettered. The exigencies of his cricket tour will compel him constantly to be gadding about, now to Philadelphia, now to Saskatchewan, anon to Onehorseville, Ga. His services, therefore, cannot be relied upon continuously. From him, accordingly, we shall expect little but moral support. An occasional congratulatory telegram. Now and then a bright smile of approval. The bulk of the work will devolve upon our two selves.'

'Let it devolve,' said Billy Windsor, enthusiastically.

'Assuredly,' said Psmith. 'And now to decide upon our main scheme. You, of course, are the editor, and my suggestions are merely suggestions, subject to your approval. But, briefly, my idea is that *Cosy Moments* should become red-hot stuff. I could wish its tone to be such that the public will wonder why we do not print it on asbestos. We must chronicle all the live events of the day, murders, fires, and the like in a manner which will make our readers' spines thrill. Above all, we must be the guardians of the People's rights. We must be a searchlight, showing up the dark spot in the souls of those who would endeavour in any way to do the PEOPLE in the eye. We must detect the wrong-doer, and deliver him such a series of resentful biffs that he will abandon his little games and become a model citizen. The details of the campaign we must think out after, but I fancy that, if we follow those main lines, we shall produce a bright, readable little sheet which will in a measure make this city sit up and take notice. Are you with me, Comrade Windsor?'

'Surest thing you know,' said Billy with fervour.

6. The Tenements

To alter the scheme of a weekly from cover to cover is not a task that is completed without work. The dismissal of *Cosy Moments'* entire staff of contributors left a gap in the paper which had to be filled, and owing to the nearness of press day there was no time to fill it before the issue of the next number. The editorial staff had to be satisfied with heading every page with the words 'Look out! Look out!! Look out!!! See foot of page!!!!' printing in the space at the bottom the legend 'Next Week! See Editorial!' and compiling in conjunction a snappy editorial, setting forth the proposed changes. This was largely the work of Psmith.

'Comrade Jackson,' he said to Mike, as they set forth one evening in search of their new flat, 'I fancy I have found my *métier*. Commerce, many considered, was the line I should take; and doubtless, had I stuck to that walk in life, I should soon have become a financial magnate. But something seemed to whisper to me, even in the midst of my triumphs in the New Asiatic Bank, that there were other fields. For the moment it seems to me that I have found the job for which nature specially designed me. At last I have Scope. And without Scope, where are we? Wedged tightly in among the ribstons. There are some very fine passages in that editorial. The last paragraph, beginning "*Cosy Moments* cannot be muzzled", in particular. I like it. It strikes the right note. It should stir the blood of a free and independent people till they sit in platoons on the doorstep of our office, waiting for the next number to appear.'

'How about the next number?' asked Mike. 'Are you and Windsor going to fill the whole paper yourselves?'

'By no means. It seems that Comrade Windsor knows certain

stout fellows, reporters on other papers, who will be delighted to weigh in with stuff for a moderate fee.'

'How about Luella What's-her-name and the others? How have they taken it?'

'Up to the present we have no means of ascertaining. The letters giving them the miss-in-baulk in no uncertain voice were only dispatched yesterday. But it cannot affect us how they writhe beneath the blow. There is no reprieve.'

Mike roared with laughter.

'It's the rummiest business I ever struck,' he said. 'I'm jolly glad it's not my paper. It's pretty lucky for you two lunatics that the proprietor's in Europe.'

Psmith regarded him with pained surprise.

'I do not understand you, Comrade Jackson. Do you insinuate that we are not acting in the proprietor's best interests? When he sees the receipts after we have handled the paper for a while, he will go singing about his hotel. His beaming smile will be a by-word in Carlsbad. Visitors will be shown it as one of the sights. His only doubt will be whether to send his money to the bank or keep it in tubs and roll in it. We are on to a big thing, Comrade Jackson. Wait till you see our first number.'

'And how about the editor? I should think that first number would bring him back foaming at the mouth.'

'I have ascertained from Comrade Windsor that there is nothing to fear from that quarter. By a singular stroke of good fortune Comrade Wilberfloss – his name is Wilberfloss – has been ordered complete rest during his holiday. The kindly medico, realizing the fearful strain inflicted by reading *Cosy Moments* in its old form, specifically mentioned that the paper was to be withheld from him until he returned.'

'And when he does return, what are you going to do?'

'By that time, doubtless, the paper will be in so flourishing a state that he will confess how wrong his own methods were and adopt ours without a murmur. In the meantime, Comrade Jackson, I would call your attention to the fact that we seem to have lost our way. In the exhilaration of this little chat, our footsteps have wandered. Where we are, goodness only knows. I can only say that I shouldn't care to have to live here.'

'There's a name up on the other side of that lamp-post.'

'Let us wend in that direction. Ah, Pleasant Street? I fancy that the master-mind who chose that name must have had the rudiments of a sense of humour.'

It was indeed a repellent neighbourhood in which they had arrived. The New York slum stands in a class of its own. It is unique. The height of the houses and the narrowness of the streets seem to condense its unpleasantness. All the smells and noises, which are many and varied, are penned up in a sort of canyon, and gain in vehemence from the fact. The masses of dirty clothes hanging from the fire-escapes increase the depression. Nowhere in the city does one realize so fully the disadvantages of a lack of space. New York, being an island, has had no room to spread. It is a town of human sardines. In the poorer quarters the congestion is unbelievable.

Psmith and Mike picked their way through the groups of ragged children who covered the roadway. There seemed to be thousands of them.

'Poor kids!' said Mike. 'It must be awful living in a hole like this.'

Psmith said nothing. He was looking thoughtful. He glanced up at the grimy buildings on each side. On the lower floors one could see into dark, bare rooms. These were the star apartments of the tenement houses, for they opened on to the street, and so got a little light and air. The imagination jibbed at the thought of the back rooms.

'I wonder who owns these places,' said Psmith. 'It seems to me that there's what you might call room for improvement. It wouldn't be a scaly idea to turn that *Cosy Moments* searchlight we were talking about on to them.'

They walked on a few steps.

'Look here,' said Psmith, stopping. 'This place makes me sick. I'm going in to have a look round. I expect some muscular householder will resent the intrusion and boot us out, but we'll risk it.'

Followed by Mike, he turned in at one of the doors. A group of men leaning against the opposite wall looked at them without curiosity. Probably they took them for reporters hunting for a story. Reporters were the only tolerably well-dressed visitors Pleasant Street ever entertained.

It was almost pitch dark on the stairs. They had to feel their way up. Most of the doors were shut but one on the second floor was ajar. Through the opening they had a glimpse of a number of women sitting round on boxes. The floor was covered with little heaps of linen. All the women were sewing. Mike, stumbling in the darkness, almost fell against the door. None of the women looked up at the noise. Time was evidently money in Pleasant Street.

On the fourth floor there was an open door. The room was empty. It was a good representative Pleasant Street back room. The architect in this case had given rein to a passion for originality. He had constructed the room without a window of any sort whatsoever. There was a square opening in the door. Through this, it was to be presumed, the entire stock of air used by the occupants was supposed to come.

They stumbled downstairs again and out into the street. By contrast with the conditions indoors the street seemed spacious and breezy.

'This,' said Psmith, as they walked on, 'is where *Cosy Moments* gets busy at a singularly early date.'

'What are you going to do?' asked Mike.

'I propose, Comrade Jackson,' said Psmith, 'if Comrade Windsor is agreeable, to make things as warm for the owner of this place as I jolly well know how. What he wants, of course,' he proceeded in the tone of a family doctor prescribing for a patient, 'is disembowelling. I fancy, however, that a mawkishly sentimental legislature will prevent our performing that national service. We must endeavour to do what we can by means of kindly criticisms in the paper. And now, having settled that important point, let us try and get out of this place of wrath, and find Fourth Avenue.'

7. Visitors at the Office

On the following morning Mike had to leave with the team for Philadelphia. Psmith came down to the ferry to see him off, and hung about moodily until the time of departure.

'It is saddening to me to a great extent, Comrade Jackson,' he said, 'this perpetual parting of the ways. When I think of the happy moments we have spent hand-in-hand across the seas, it fills me with a certain melancholy to have you flitting off in this manner without me. Yet there is another side to the picture. To me there is something singularly impressive in our unhesitating reply to the calls of Duty. Your Duty summons you to Philadelphia, to knock the cover off the local bowling. Mine retains me here, to play my part in the great work of making New York sit up. By the time you return, with a century or two, I trust, in your bag, the good work should, I fancy, be getting something of a move on. I will complete the arrangements with regard to the flat.'

After leaving Pleasant Street they had found Fourth Avenue by a devious route, and had opened negotiations for a large flat near Thirtieth Street. It was immediately above a saloon, which was something of a drawback, but the landlord had assured them that the voices of the revellers did not penetrate to it.

When the ferry-boat had borne Mike off across the river, Psmith turned to stroll to the office of *Cosy Moments*. The day was fine, and on the whole, despite Mike's desertion, he felt pleased with life. Psmith's was a nature which required a certain amount of stimulus in the way of gentle excitement; and it seemed to him that the conduct of the remodelled *Cosy Moments* might supply this. He liked Billy Windsor, and looked forward to a not unenjoyable time till Mike should return.

The offices of *Cosy Moments* were in a large building in the street off Madison Avenue. They consisted of a sort of outer lair, where Pugsy Maloney spent his time reading tales of life in the prairies and heading off undesirable visitors; a small room, which would have belonged to the stenographer if *Cosy Moments* had possessed one; and a larger room beyond, which was the editorial sanctum.

As Psmith passed through the front door, Pugsy Maloney rose.

'Say!' said Master Maloney.

'Say on, Comrade Maloney,' said Psmith.

'Dey're in dere.'

'Who, precisely?'

'A whole bunch of dem.'

Psmith inspected Master Maloney through his eye-glass. 'Can you give me any particulars?' he asked patiently. 'You are well-meaning, but vague, Comrade Maloney. Who are in there?'

'De whole bunch of dem. Dere's Mr Asher and the Rev. Philpotts and a gazebo what calls himself Waterman and about 'steen more of dem.'

A faint smile appeared upon Psmith's face.

'And is Comrade Windsor in there, too, in the middle of them?'

'Nope. Mr Windsor's out to lunch.'

'Comrade Windsor knows his business. Why did you let them in?'

'Sure, dey just butted in,' said Master Maloney complainingly. 'I was sittin' here, readin' me book, when de foist of de guys blew in. "Boy," says he, "is de editor in?" "Nope," I says. "I'll go in an' wait," says he. "Nuttin' doing", says I. "Nix on de goin' in act." I might as well have saved me breat'. In he butts, and he's in der now. Well, in about t'ree minutes along comes another gazebo. "Boy," said he, "is de editor in?" "Nope," I says. "I'll wait," says he lightin' out for de door. Wit dat I sees de proposition's too fierce for muh. I can't keep dese big husky guys out if dey's for buttin' in. So when de rest of de bunch comes along, I don't try to give dem de t'run down. I says, "Well, gents," I says, "it's up to youse. De editor ain't in,

39

but if youse wants to join de giddy t'rong, push t'roo inter de inner room. I can't be boddered." '

'And what more *could* you have said?' agreed Psmith approvingly. 'Tell me, Comrade Maloney, what was the general average aspect of these determined spirits?'

'Huh?'

'Did they seem to you to be gay, lighthearted? Did they carol snatches of song as they went? Or did they appear to be looking for someone with a hatchet?'

'Dey was hoppin'-mad, de whole bunch of dem.'

'As I suspected. But we must not repine, Comrade Maloney. These trifling *contretemps* are the penalties we pay for our high journalistic aims. I will interview these merchants. I fancy that with the aid of the Diplomatic Smile and the Honeyed Word I may manage to pull through. It is as well, perhaps, that Comrade Windsor is out. The situation calls for the handling of a man of delicate culture and nice tact. Comrade Windsor would probably have endeavoured to clear the room with a chair. If he should arrive during the *séance*, Comrade Maloney, be so good as to inform him of the state of affairs, and tell him not to come in. Give him my compliments, and tell him to go out and watch the snowdrops growing in Madison Square Garden.'

'Sure,' said Master Maloney.

Then Psmith, having smoothed the nap of his hat and flicked a speck of dust from his coat-sleeve, walked to the door of the inner room and went in.

8. The Honeyed Word

Master Maloney's statement that 'about 'steen visitors' had arrived in addition to Messrs Asher, Waterman, and the Rev. Philpotts proved to have been due to a great extent to a somewhat feverish imagination. There were only five men in the room.

As Psmith entered, every eye was turned upon him. To an outside spectator he would have seemed rather like a very well-dressed Daniel introduced into a den of singularly irritable lions. Five pairs of eyes were smouldering with a long-nursed resentment. Five brows were corrugated with wrathful lines. Such, however, was the simple majesty of Psmith's demeanour that for a moment there was a dead silence. Not a word was spoken as he paced, wrapped in thought, to the editorial chair. Stillness brooded over the room as he carefully dusted that piece of furniture, and, having done so to his satisfaction, hitched up the knees of his trousers and sank gracefully into a sitting position.

This accomplished, he looked up and started. He gazed round the room.

'Ha! I am observed!' he murmured.

The words broke the spell. Instantly, the five visitors burst simultaneously into speech.

'Are you the acting editor of this paper?'

'I wish to have a word with you, sir.'

'Mr Windsor, I presume?'

'Pardon me!'

'I should like a few moments' conversation.'

The start was good and even; but the gentleman who said 'Pardon me!' necessarily finished first with the rest nowhere.

Psmith turned to him, bowed, and fixed him with a benevolent gaze through his eye-glass.

'Are you Mr Windsor, sir, may I ask?' inquired the favoured one.

The others paused for the reply.

'Alas! no,' said Psmith with manly regret.

'Then who are you?'

'I am Psmith.'

There was a pause.

'Where is Mr Windsor?'

'He is, I fancy, champing about forty cents' worth of lunch at some neighbouring hostelry.'

'When will he return?'

'Anon. But how much anon I fear I cannot say.'

The visitors looked at each other.

'This is exceedingly annoying,' said the man who had said 'Pardon me!' 'I came for the express purpose of seeing Mr Windsor.'

'So did I,' chimed in the rest. 'Same here. So did I.'

Psmith bowed courteously.

'Comrade Windsor's loss is my gain. Is there anything I can do for you?'

'Are you on the editorial staff of this paper?'

'I am acting sub-editor. The work is not light,' added Psmith gratuitously. 'Sometimes the cry goes round, "Can Psmith get through it all? Will his strength support his unquenchable spirit?" But I stagger on. I do not repine. I – '

'Then maybe you can tell me what all this means?' said a small round gentleman who so far had done only chorus work.

'If it is in my power to do so, it shall be done, Comrade – I have not the pleasure of your name?'

'My name is Waterman, sir. I am here on behalf of my wife, whose name you doubtless know.'

'Correct me if I am wrong,' said Psmith, 'but I should say it, also, was Waterman.'

'Luella Granville Waterman, sir,' said the little man proudly. Psmith removed his eye-glass, polished it, and replaced it in his eye. He felt that he must run no risk of not seeing clearly the husband of one who, in his opinion, stood alone in literary circles as a purveyor of sheer bilge.

'My wife,' continued the little man, producing an envelope and handing it to Psmith, 'has received this extraordinary communication from a man signing himself W. Windsor. We are both at a loss to make head or tail of it.'

Psmith was reading the letter.

'It seems reasonably clear to me,' he said.

'It is an outrage. My wife has been a contributor to this journal from its foundation. Her work has given every satisfaction to Mr Wilberfloss. And now, without the slightest warning, comes this peremptory dismissal from W. Windsor. Who is W. Windsor? Where is Mr Wilberfloss?'

The chorus burst forth. It seemed that that was what they all wanted to know: Who was W. Windsor? Where was Mr Wilberfloss?

'I am the Reverend Edwin T. Philpotts, sir,' said a cadaverous-looking man with pale blue eyes and a melancholy face. 'I have contributed "Moments of Meditation" to this journal for a very considerable period of time.'

'I have read your page with the keenest interest,' said Psmith. 'I may be wrong, but yours seems to me work which the world will not willingly let die.'

The Reverend Edwin's frosty face thawed into a bleak smile.

'And yet,' continued Psmith, 'I gather that Comrade Windsor, on the other hand, actually wishes to hurry on its decease. It is these strange contradictions, these clashings of personal taste, which make up what we call life. Here we have, on the one hand – '

A man with a face like a walnut, who had hitherto lurked almost unseen behind a stout person in a serge suit, bobbed into the open, and spoke his piece.

'Where's this fellow Windsor? W. Windsor. That's the man we want to see. I've been working for this paper without a break, except when I had the mumps, for four years, and I've reason to know that my page was as widely read and appreciated as any in New York. And now up comes this Windsor fellow, if you please, and tells me in so many words the paper's got no use for me.'

'These are life's tragedies,' murmured Psmith.

'What's he mean by it? That's what I want to know. And that's what these gentlemen want to know – See here – '

'I am addressing – ?' said Psmith.

'Asher's my name. B. Henderson Asher. I write "Moments of Mirth".'

A look almost of excitement came into Psmith's face, such a look as a visitor to a foreign land might wear when confronted with some great national monument. That he should be privileged to look upon the author of 'Moments of Mirth' in the flesh, face to face, was almost too much.

'Comrade Asher,' he said reverently, 'may I shake your hand?'

The other extended his hand with some suspicion.

'Your "Moments of Mirth",' said Psmith, shaking it, 'have frequently reconciled me to the toothache.'

He reseated himself.

'Gentlemen,' he said, 'this is a painful case. The circumstances, as you will readily admit when you have heard all, are peculiar. You have asked me where Mr Wilberfloss is. I do not know.'

'You don't know!' exclaimed Mr Waterman.

'I don't know. You don't know. They,' said Psmith, indicating the rest with a wave of the hand, 'don't know. Nobody knows. His locality is as hard to ascertain as that of a black cat in a coal-cellar on a moonless night. Shortly before I joined this journal, Mr Wilberfloss, by his doctor's orders, started out on a holiday, leaving no address. No letters were to be forwarded. He was to enjoy complete rest. Where is he now? Who shall say? Possibly legging it down some rugged slope in the Rockies, with two bears and a wild cat in earnest pursuit. Possibly in the midst of some Florida everglade, making a noise like a piece of meat in order to snare crocodiles. Possibly in Canada, baiting moose-traps. We have no data.'

Silent consternation prevailed among the audience. Finally the Rev. Edwin T. Philpotts was struck with an idea.

'Where is Mr White?' he asked.

The point was well received.

'Yes, where's Mr Benjamin White?' chorused the rest.

Psmith shook his head.

'In Europe. I cannot say more.'

The audience's consternation deepened.

'Then, do you mean to say,' demanded Mr Asher, 'that this fellow Windsor's the boss here, that what he says goes?'

Psmith bowed.

'With your customary clear-headedness, Comrade Asher, you have got home on the bull's-eye first pop. Comrade Windsor is indeed the boss. A man of intensely masterful character, he will brook no opposition. I am powerless to sway him. Suggestions from myself as to the conduct of the paper would infuriate him. He believes that radical changes are necessary in the programme of *Cosy Moments,* and he means to put them through if it snows. Doubtless he would gladly consider your work if it fitted in with his ideas. A snappy account of a glove-fight, a spine-shaking word picture of a railway smash, or something on those lines, would be welcomed. But – '

'I have never heard of such a thing,' said Mr Waterman indignantly.

Psmith sighed.

'Some time ago,' he said, ' – how long it seems! – I remember saying to a young friend of mine of the name of Spiller, "Comrade Spiller, never confuse the unusual with the impossible." It is my guiding rule in life. It is unusual for the substitute-editor of a weekly paper to do a Captain Kidd act and take entire command of the journal on his own account; but is it impossible? Alas no. Comrade Windsor has done it. That is where you, Comrade Asher, and you, gentlemen, have landed yourselves squarely in the broth. You have confused the unusual with the impossible.'

'But what is to be done?' cried Mr Asher.

'I fear that there is nothing to be done, except wait. The present *régime* is but an experiment. It may be that when Comrade Wilberfloss, having dodged the bears and eluded the wild cat, returns to his post at the helm of this journal he may decide not to continue on the lines at present mapped out. He should be back in about ten weeks.'

'Ten weeks!'

'I fancy that was to be the duration of his holiday. Till then my advice to you gentlemen is to wait. You may rely on me to keep a watchful eye upon your interests. When your thoughts tend to take a gloomy turn, say to yourselves, "All is well. Psmith is keeping a watchful eye upon our interests." '

'All the same, I should like to see this W. Windsor,' said Mr Asher.

Psmith shook his head.

'I shouldn't,' he said. 'I speak in your best interests. Comrade Windsor is a man of the fiercest passions. He cannot brook interference. Were you to question the wisdom of his plans, there is no knowing what might not happen. He would be the first to regret any violent action, when once he had cooled off, but would that be any consolation to his victim? I think not. Of course, if you wish it, I could arrange a meeting – '

Mr Asher said no, he thought it didn't matter.

'I guess I can wait,' he said.

'That,' said Psmith approvingly, 'is the right spirit. Wait. That is the watch-word. And now,' he added, rising, 'I wonder if a bit of lunch somewhere might not be a good thing? We have had an interesting but fatiguing little chat. Our tissues require restoring. If you gentlemen would care to join me – '

Ten minutes later the company was seated in complete harmony round a table at the Knickerbocker. Psmith, with the dignified bonhomie of a seigneur of the old school was ordering the wine; while B. Henderson Asher, brimming over with good-humour, was relating to an attentive circle an anecdote which should have appeared in his next instalment of 'Moments of Mirth'.

9. Full Steam Ahead

When Psmith returned to the office, he found Billy Windsor in the doorway, just parting from a thick-set young man, who seemed to be expressing his gratitude to the editor for some good turn. He was shaking him warmly by the hand.

Psmith stood aside to let him pass.

'An old college chum, Comrade Windsor?' he asked.

'That was Kid Brady.'

'The name is unfamiliar to me. Another contributor?'

'He's from my part of the country – Wyoming. He wants to fight anyone in the world at a hundred and thirty-three pounds.'

'We all have our hobbies. Comrade Brady appears to have selected a somewhat exciting one. He would find stamp-collecting less exacting.'

'It hasn't given him much excitement so far, poor chap,' said Billy Windsor. 'He's in the championship class, and here he has been pottering about New York for a month without being able to get a fight. It's always the way in this rotten East,' continued Billy, warming up as was his custom when discussing a case of oppression and injustice. 'It's all graft here. You've got to let half a dozen brutes dip into every dollar you earn, or you don't get a chance. If the kid had a manager, he'd get all the fights he wanted. And the manager would get nearly all the money. I've told him that we will back him up.'

'You have hit it, Comrade Windsor,' said Psmith with enthusiasm. '*Cosy Moments* shall be Comrade Brady's manager. We will give him a much-needed boost up in our columns. A sporting section is what the paper requires more than anything.'

'If things go on as they've started, what it will require still more will be a fighting-editor. Pugsy tells me you had visitors while I was out.'

'A few,' said Psmith. 'One or two very entertaining fellows. Comrades Asher, Philpotts, and others. I have just been giving them a bite of lunch at the Knickerbocker.'

'Lunch!'

'A most pleasant little lunch. We are now as brothers. I fear I have made you perhaps a shade unpopular with our late contributors; but these things must be. We must clench our teeth and face them manfully. If I were you, I think I should not drop in at the house of Comrade Asher and the rest to take pot-luck for some little time to come. In order to soothe the squad I was compelled to curse you to some extent.'

'Don't mind me.'

'I think I may say I didn't.'

'Say, look here, you must charge up the price of that lunch to the office. Necessary expenses, you know.'

'I could not dream of doing such a thing, Comrade Windsor. The whole affair was a great treat to me. I have few pleasures. Comrade Asher alone was worth the money. I found his society intensely interesting. I have always believed in the Darwinian theory. Comrade Asher confirmed my views.'

They went into the inner office. Psmith removed his hat and coat.

'And now once more to work,' he said. 'Psmith the *flaneur* of Fifth Avenue ceases to exist. In his place we find Psmith the hard-headed sub-editor. Be so good as to indicate a job of work for me, Comrade Windsor. I am champing at my bit.'

Billy Windsor sat down, and lit his pipe.

'What we want most,' he said thoughtfully, 'is some big topic. That's the only way to get a paper going. Look at *Everybody's Magazine*. They didn't amount to a row of beans till Lawson started his "Frenzied Finance" articles. Directly they began, the whole country was squealing for copies. *Everybody's* put up their price from ten to fifteen cents, and now they lead the field.'

'The country must squeal for *Cosy Moments*,' said Psmith firmly. 'I fancy I have a scheme which may not prove wholly scaly. Wandering yesterday with Comrade Jackson in a search for Fourth Avenue, I happened upon a spot called Pleasant Street. Do you know it?'

Billy Windsor nodded.

'I went down there once or twice when I was a reporter. It's a beastly place.'

'It is a singularly beastly place. We went into one of the houses.'

'They're pretty bad.'

'Who owns them?'

'I don't know. Probably some millionaire. Those tenement houses are about as paying an investment as you can have.'

'Hasn't anybody ever tried to do anything about them?'

'Not so far as I know. It's pretty difficult to get at these fellows, you see. But they're fierce, aren't they, those houses!'

'What,' asked Psmith, 'is the precise difficulty of getting at these merchants?'

'Well, it's this way. There are all sorts of laws about the places, but anyone who wants can get round them as easy as falling off a log. The law says a tenement house is a building occupied by more than two families. Well, when there's a fuss, all the man has to do is to clear out all the families but two. Then, when the inspector fellow comes along, and says, let's say, "Where's your running water on each floor? That's what the law says you've got to have, and here are these people having to go downstairs and out of doors to fetch their water supplies," the landlord simply replies, "Nothing doing. This isn't a tenement house at all. There are only two families here." And when the fuss has blown over, back come the rest of the crowd, and things go on the same as before.'

'I see,' said Psmith. 'A very cheery scheme.'

'Then there's another thing. You can't get hold of the man who's really responsible, unless you're prepared to spend thousands ferreting out evidence. The land belongs in the first place to some corporation or other. They lease it to a lessee. When there's a fuss, they say they aren't responsible, it's up to the lessee. And he lies so low that you can't find out who he is. It's all just like the East. Everything in the East is as crooked as

Pearl Street. If you want a square deal, you've got to come out Wyoming way.'

'The main problem, then,' said Psmith, 'appears to be the discovery of the lessee, lad? Surely a powerful organ like *Cosy Moments,* with its vast ramifications, could bring off a thing like that?'

'I doubt it. We'll try, anyway. There's no knowing but what we may have luck.'

'Precisely,' said Psmith. 'Full steam ahead, and trust to luck. The chances are that, if we go on long enough, we shall eventually arrive somewhere. After all, Columbus didn't know that America existed when he set out. All he knew was some highly interesting fact about an egg. What that was, I do not at the moment recall, but it bucked Columbus up like a tonic. It made him fizz ahead like a two-year-old. The facts which will nerve us to effort are two. In the first place, we know that there must be someone at the bottom of the business. Secondly, as there appears to be no law of libel whatsoever in this great and free country, we shall be enabled to haul up our slacks with a considerable absence of restraint.'

'Sure,' said Billy Windsor. 'Which of us is going to write the first article?'

'You may leave it to me, Comrade Windsor. I am no hardened old journalist, I fear, but I have certain qualifications for the post. A young man once called at the office of a certain newspaper, and asked for a job. "Have you any special line?" asked the editor. "Yes," said the bright lad, "I am rather good at invective." "Any special kind of invective?" queried the man up top. "No," replied our hero, "just general invective." Such is my own case, Comrade Windsor. I am a very fair purveyor of good, general invective. And as my visit to Pleasant Street is of such recent date, I am tolerably full of my subject. Taking full advantage of the benevolent laws of this country govering libel, I fancy I will produce a screed which will make this anonymous lessee feel as if he had inadvertently seated himself upon a tintack. Give me pen and paper, Comrade Windsor, instruct Comrade Maloney to suspend his whistling till such time as I am better able to listen to it; and I think we have got a success.'

10. Going Some

There was once an editor of a paper in the Far West who was sitting at his desk, musing pleasantly of life, when a bullet crashed through the window and embedded itself in the wall at the back of his head. A happy smile lit up the editor's face. 'Ah,' he said complacently, 'I knew that Personal column of ours was going to be a success!'

What the bullet was to the Far West editor, the visit of Mr Francis Parker to the offices of *Cosy Moments* was to Billy Windsor.

It occurred in the third week of the new *régime* of the paper. *Cosy Moments*, under its new management, had bounded ahead like a motor-car when the throttle is opened. Incessant work had been the order of the day. Billy Windsor's hair had become more dishevelled than ever, and even Psmith had at moments lost a certain amount of his dignified calm. Sandwiched in between the painful case of Kid Brady and the matter of the tenements, which formed the star items of the paper's contents, was a mass of bright reading dealing with the events of the day. Billy Windsor's newspaper friends had turned in some fine, snappy stuff in their best Yellow Journal manner, relating to the more stirring happenings in the city. Psmith, who had constituted himself guardian of the literary and dramatic interests of the paper, had employed his gift of general invective to considerable effect, as was shown by a conversation between Master Maloney and a visitor one morning, heard through the open door.

'I wish to see the editor of this paper,' said the visitor.

'Editor not in,' said Master Maloney, untruthfully.

'Ha! Then when he returns I wish you to give him a message.'

'Sure.'

'I am Aubrey Bodkin, of the National Theatre. Give him my compliments, and tell him that Mr Bodkin does not lightly forget.'

An unsolicited testimonial which caused Psmith the keenest satisfaction.

The section of the paper devoted to Kid Brady was attractive to all those with sporting blood in them. Each week there appeared in the same place on the same page a portrait of the Kid, looking moody and important, in an attitude of self-defence, and under the portrait the legend, 'Jimmy Garvin must meet this boy'. Jimmy was the present holder of the light-weight title. He had won it a year before, and since then had confined himself to smoking cigars as long as walking-sticks and appearing nightly as the star in a music-hall sketch entitled 'A Fight for Honour'. His reminiscences were appearing weekly in a Sunday paper. It was this that gave Psmith the idea of publishing Kid Brady's autobiography in *Cosy Moments,* an idea which made the Kid his devoted adherent from then on. Like most pugilists, the Kid had a passion for bursting into print, and his life had been saddened up to the present by the refusal of the press to publish his reminiscences. To appear in print is the fighter's accolade. It signifies that he has arrived. Psmith extended the hospitality of page four of *Cosy Moments* to Kid Brady, and the latter leaped at the chance. He was grateful to Psmith for not editing his contributions. Other pugilists, contributing to other papers, groaned under the supervision of a member of the staff who cut out their best passages and altered the rest into Addisonian English. The readers of *Cosy Moments* got Kid Brady raw.

'Comrade Brady,' said Psmith to Billy, 'has a singularly pure and pleasing style. It is bound to appeal powerfully to the many-headed. Listen to this bit. Our hero is fighting Battling Jack Benson in that eminent artist's native town of Louisville, and the citizens have given their native son the Approving Hand, while receiving Comrade Brady with chilly silence. Here is the Kid on the subject: "I looked around that house, and I seen I hadn't a friend in it. And then the gong goes, and I says to myself how I has one friend, my poor old mother way out in Wyoming, and I goes in and mixes it, and then I seen Benson losing his goat, so I ups with an awful half-scissor hook to the plexus, and in the next round I see Benson has a chunk of yellow, and I gets in with a hay-maker and I picks up another sleep-producer from the floor and hands it him, and he takes the count all right.' ... Crisp, lucid, and to the point. That is what the public wants. If this does not bring Comrade Garvin up to the scratch, nothing will.'

But the feature of the paper was the 'Tenement' series. It was late summer now, and there was nothing much going on in New York. The public was consequently free to take notice. The sale of *Cosy Moments* proceeded briskly. As Psmith had predicted, the change of policy had the effect of improving the sales to a marked extent. Letters of complaint from old subscribers poured into the office daily. But, as Billy Windsor complacently remarked, they had paid their subscriptions, so that the money was safe whether they read the paper or not. And, meanwhile, a large new public had sprung up and was growing every week. Advertisements came trooping in. *Cosy Moments*, in short, was passing through an era of prosperity undreamed of in its history.

'Young blood,' said Psmith nonchalantly, 'young blood. That is the secret. A paper must keep up to date, or it falls behind its competitors in the race. Comrade Wilberfloss's methods were possibly sound, but too limited and archaic. They lacked ginger. We of the younger generation have our fingers more firmly on the public pulse. We read off the public's unspoken wishes as if by intuition. We know the game from A to Z.'

At this moment Master Maloney entered, bearing in his hand a card.

' "Francis Parker"?' said Billy taking it. 'Don't know him.'

'Nor I,' said Psmith. 'We make new friends daily.'

'He's a guy with a tall-shaped hat,' volunteered Master Maloney, 'an' he's wearin' a dude suit an' shiny shoes.'

'Comrade Parker,' said Psmith approvingly, 'has evidently not been blind to the importance of a visit to *Cosy Moments*. He has dressed himself in his best. He has felt, rightly, that this is no occasion for the old straw hat and the baggy flannels. I would not have it otherwise. It is the right spirit. Shall we give him audience, Comrade Windsor?'

'I wonder what he wants.'

'That,' said Psmith, 'we shall ascertain more clearly after a personal interview. Comrade Maloney, show the gentleman in. We can give him three and a quarter minutes.'

Pugsy withdrew.

Mr Francis Parker proved to be a man who might have been any age between twenty-five and thirty-five. He had a smooth, clean-shaven face, and a cat-like way of moving. As Pugsy had stated in effect, he wore a tail-coat, trousers with a crease which brought a smile of kindly approval to Psmith's face, and patent-leather boots of pronounced shininess. Gloves and a tall hat, which he carried, completed an impressive picture.

He moved softly into the room.

'I wished to see the editor.'

Psmith waved a hand towards Billy.

'The treat has not been denied you,' he said. 'Before you is Comrade Windsor, the Wyoming cracker-jack. He is our editor. I myself – I am Psmith – though but a subordinate, may also claim the title in a measure. Technically, I am but a sub-editor; but such is the mutual esteem in which Comrade Windsor and I hold each other that we may practically be said to be inseparable. We have no secrets from each other. You may address us both impartially. Will you sit for a space?'

He pushed a chair towards the visitor, who seated himself with the care inspired by a perfect trouser-crease. There was a momentary silence while he selected a spot on the table on which to place his hat.

'The style of the paper has changed greatly, has it not, during the past few weeks?' he said. 'I have never been, shall I say, a constant reader of *Cosy Moments,* and I may be wrong. But is not its interest in current affairs a recent development?'

'You are very right,' responded Psmith. 'Comrade Windsor, a man of alert and restless temperament, felt that a change was essential if *Cosy Moments* was to lead public thought. Comrade Wilberfloss's methods were good in their way. I have no quarrel with Comrade Wilberfloss. But he did not lead public thought. He catered exclusively for children with water on the brain, and men and women with solid ivory skulls. Comrade Windsor, with a broader view, feels that there are other and larger publics. He refuses to content himself with ladling out a weekly dole of mental predigested breakfast food. He provides meat. He –'

'Then – excuse me –' said Mr Parker, turning to Billy, 'you, I take it, are responsible for this very vigorous attack on the tenement-house owners?'

'You can take it I am,' said Billy.

Psmith interposed.

'We are both responsible, Comrade Parker. If any husky guy, as I fancy Master Maloney would phrase it, is anxious to aim a swift kick at the man behind those articles, he must distribute it evenly between Comrade Windsor and myself.'

'I see.' Mr Parker paused. 'They are – er – very outspoken articles,' he added.

'Warm stuff,' agreed Psmith. 'Distinctly warm stuff.'

'May I speak frankly?' said Mr Parker.

'Assuredly, Comrade Parker. There must be no secrets, no restraint between us. We would not have you go away and say to yourself, "Did I make my meaning clear? Was I too elusive?" Say on.'

'I am speaking in your best interests.'

'Who would doubt it, Comrade Parker. Nothing has buoyed us up more strongly during the hours of doubt through which we have passed than the knowledge that you wish us well.'

Billy Windsor suddenly became militant. There was a feline smoothness about the visitor which had been jarring upon him ever since he first spoke. Billy was of the plains, the home of blunt speech, where you looked your man in the eye and said it quick. Mr Parker was too bland for human consumption. He offended Billy's honest soul.

'See here,' cried he, leaning forward, 'what's it all about? Let's have it. If you've anything to say about those articles, say it right out. Never mind our best interests. We can look after them. Let's have what's worrying you.'

Psmith waved a deprecating hand.

'Do not let us be abrupt on this happy occasion. To me it is enough simply to sit and chat with Comrade Parker, irrespective of the trend of his conversation. Still, as time is money, and this is our busy day, possibly it might be as well, sir, if you unburdened yourself as soon as convenient. Have you come to point out some flaws in those articles? Do they fall short in any way of your standard for such work?'

Mr Parker's smooth face did not change its expression, but he came to the point.

'I should not go on with them if I were you,' he said.

'Why?' demanded Billy.

'There are reasons why you should not,' said Mr Parker.

'And there are reasons why we should.'

'Less powerful ones.'

There proceeded from Billy a noise not describable in words. It was partly a snort, partly a growl. It resembled more than anything else the preliminary sniffing snarl a bull-dog emits before he joins battle. Billy's cowboy blood was up. He was rapidly approaching the state of mind in which the men of the plains, finding speech unequal to the expression of their thoughts, reach for their guns.

Psmith intervened.

'We do not completely gather your meaning, Comrade Parker. I fear we must ask you to hand it to us with still more breezy frankness. Do you speak from purely friendly motives? Are you advising us to discontinue the articles merely because you fear that they will damage our literary reputation? Or are there other reasons why you feel that they should cease? Do you speak solely as a literary connoisseur? Is it the style or the subject-matter of which you disapprove?'

Mr Parker leaned forward.

'The gentleman whom I represent – '

'Then this is no matter of your own personal taste? You are an emissary?'

'These articles are causing a certain inconvenience to the gentleman whom I represent. Or, rather, he feels that, if continued, they may do so.'

'You mean,' broke in Billy explosively, 'that if we kick up

enough fuss to make somebody start a commission to inquire into this rotten business, your friend who owns the private Hades we're trying to get improved, will have to get busy and lose some of his money by making the houses fit to live in? Is that it?'

'It is not so much the money, Mr Windsor, though, of course, the expense would be considerable. My employer is a wealthy man.'

'I bet he is,' said Billy disgustedly. 'I've no doubt he makes a mighty good pile out of Pleasant Street.'

'It is not so much the money,' repeated Mr Parker, 'as the publicity involved. I speak quite frankly. There are reasons why my employer would prefer not to come before the public just now as the owner of the Pleasant Street property. I need not go into those reasons. It is sufficient to say that they are strong ones.'

'Well, he knows what to do, I guess. The moment he starts to make those houses decent, the articles stop. It's up to him.'

Psmith nodded.

'Comrade Windsor is correct. He has hit the mark and rung the bell. No conscientious judge would withhold from Comrade Windsor a cigar or a coconut, according as his private preference might dictate. That is the matter in a nutshell. Remove the reason for those very scholarly articles, and they cease.'

Mr Parker shook his head.

'I fear that is not feasible. The expense of reconstructing the houses makes that impossible.'

'Then there's no use in talking,' said Billy. 'The articles will go on.'

Mr Parker coughed. A tentative cough, suggesting that the situation was now about to enter upon a more delicate phase. Billy and Psmith waited for him to begin. From their point of view the discussion was over. If it was to be reopened on fresh lines, it was for their visitor to effect that reopening.

'Now, I'm going to be frank, gentlemen,' said he, as who should say, 'We are all friends here. Let us be hearty.' 'I'm going to put my cards on the table, and see if we can't fix something up. Now, see here. We don't want unpleasantness.

You aren't in this business for your healths, eh? You've got your living to make, just like everybody else, I guess. Well, see here. This is how it stands. To a certain extent, I don't mind admitting, seeing that we're being frank with one another, you two gentlemen have got us – that's to say, my employer – in a cleft stick. Frankly, those articles are beginning to attract attention, and if they go on there's going to be a lot of inconvenience for my employer. That's clear, I reckon. Well, now, here's a square proposition. How much do you want to stop those articles? That's straight. I've been frank with you, and I want you to be frank with me. What's your figure? Name it, and, if it's not too high, I guess we needn't quarrel.'

He looked expectantly at Billy. Billy's eyes were bulging. He struggled for speech. He had got as far as 'Say!' when Psmith interrupted him. Psmith, gazing sadly at Mr Parker through his monocle, spoke quietly, with the restrained dignity of some old Roman senator dealing with the enemies of the Republic.

'Comrade Parker,' he said, 'I fear that you have allowed constant communication with the conscienceless commercialism of this worldly city to undermine your moral sense. It is useless to dangle rich bribes before our eyes. *Cosy Moments* cannot be muzzled. You doubtless mean well, according to your – if I may say so – somewhat murky lights, but we are not for sale, except at ten cents weekly. From the hills of Maine to the Everglades of Florida, from Sandy Hook to San Francisco, from Portland, Oregon, to Melonsquashville, Tennessee, one sentence is in every man's mouth. And what is that sentence? I give you three guesses. You give it up? It is this: "*Cosy Moments* cannot be muzzled!"'

Mr Parker rose.

'There's nothing more to be done then,' he said.

'Nothing,' agreed Psmith, 'except to make a noise like a hoop and roll away.'

'And do it quick,' yelled Billy, exploding like a fire-cracker.

Psmith bowed.

'Speed,' he admitted, 'would be no bad thing. Frankly – if I may borrow the expression – your square proposition has wounded us. I am a man of powerful self-restraint, one of those strong, silent men, and I can curb my emotions. But I fear that Comrade Windsor's generous temperament may at any moment prompt him to start throwing ink-pots. And in Wyoming his deadly aim with the ink-pot won him among the admiring cowboys the sobriquet of Crack-Shot Cuthbert. As man to man, Comrade Parker, I should advise you to bound swiftly away.'

'I'm going,' said Mr Parker, picking up his hat. 'And I'll give you a piece of advice, too. Those articles are going to be stopped, and if you've any sense between you, you'll stop them yourselves before you get hurt. That's all I've got to say, and that goes.'

He went out, closing the door behind him with a bang that added emphasis to his words.

'To men of nicely poised nervous organization such as ourselves, Comrade Windsor,' said Psmith, smoothing his waistcoat thoughtfully, 'these scenes are acutely painful. We wince before them. Our ganglions quiver like cinematographs. Gradually recovering command of ourselves, we review the situation. Did our visitor's final remarks convey anything definite to you? Were they the mere casual badinage of a parting guest, or was there something solid behind them?'

Billy Windsor was looking serious.

'I guess he meant it all right. He's evidently working for somebody pretty big, and that sort of man would have a pull with all kinds of Thugs. We shall have to watch out. Now that they find we can't be bought, they'll try the other way. They mean business sure enough. But, by George, let 'em! We're up against a big thing, and I'm going to see it through if they put every gang in New York on to us.'

'Precisely, Comrade Windsor. *Cosy Moments*, as I have had occasion to observe before, cannot be muzzled.'

'That's right,' said Billy Windsor. 'And,' he added, with the contented look the Far West editor must have worn as the bullet came through the window, 'we must have got them scared, or they wouldn't have shown their hand that way. I guess we're making a hit. *Cosy Moments* is going some now.'

11. The Man at the Astor

The duties of Master Pugsy Maloney at the offices of *Cosy Moments* were not heavy; and he was accustomed to occupy his large store of leisure by reading narratives dealing with life in the prairies, which he acquired at a neighbouring shop at cut rates in consideration of their being shop-soiled. It was while he was engrossed in one of these, on the morning following the visit of Mr Parker, that the seedy-looking man made his appearance. He walked in from the street, and stood before Master Maloney.

'Hey, kid,' he said.

Pugsy looked up with some hauteur. He resented being addressed as 'kid' by perfect strangers.

'Editor in, Tommy?' inquired the man.

Pugsy by this time had taken a thorough dislike to him. To be called 'kid' was bad. The subtle insult of 'Tommy' was still worse.

'Nope,' he said curtly, fixing his eyes again on his book. A movement on the part of the visitor attracted his attention. The seedy man was making for the door of the inner room. Pugsy instantly ceased to be the student and became the man of action. He sprang from his seat and wriggled in between the man and the door.

'Youse can't butt in dere,' he said authoritatively. 'Chase yerself.'

The man eyed him with displeasure.

'Fresh kid!' he observed disapprovingly.

'Fade away,' urged Master Maloney.

The visitor's reply was to extend a hand and grasp Pugsy's left ear between a long finger and thumb. Since time began, small boys in every country have had but one answer for this action. Pugsy made it. He emitted a piercing squeal in which pain, fear, and resentment strove for supremacy.

The noise penetrated into the editorial sanctum, losing only a small part of its strength on the way. Psmith, who was at work on a review of a book of poetry, looked up with patient sadness.

'If Comrade Maloney,' he said, 'is going to take to singing as well as whistling, I fear this journal must put up its shutters. Concentrated thought will be out of the question.'

A second squeal rent the air. Billy Windsor jumped up.

'Somebody must be hurting the kid,' he exclaimed.

He hurried to the door and flung it open. Psmith followed at a more leisurely pace. The seedy man, caught in the act, released Master Maloney, who stood rubbing his ear with resentment written on every feature.

On such occasions as this Billy was a man of few words. He made a dive for the seedy man; but the latter, who during the preceding moment had been eyeing the two editors as if he were committing their appearance to memory, sprang back, and was off down the stairs with the agility of a Marathon runner.

'He blows in,' said Master Maloney, aggrieved, 'and asks is de editor dere. I tells him no, 'cos youse said youse wasn't, and he nips me by the ear when I gets busy to stop him gettin' t'roo.'

'Comrade Maloney,' said Psmith, 'you are a martyr. What would Horatius have done if somebody had nipped him by the ear when he was holding the bridge? The story does not consider the possibility. Yet it might have made all the difference. Did the gentleman state his business?'

'Nope. Just tried to butt t'roo.'

'Another of these strong silent men. The world is full of us. These are the perils of the journalistic life. You will be safer and happier when you are rounding up cows on your mustang.'

'I wonder what he wanted,' said Billy, when they were back again in the inner room.

'Who can say, Comrade Windsor? Possibly our autographs. Possibly five minutes' chat on general subjects.'

'I don't like the look of him,' said Billy.

'Whereas what Comrade Maloney objected to was the feel of him. In what respect did his look jar upon you? His clothes were poorly cut, but such things, I know, leave you unmoved.'

'It seems to me,' said Billy thoughtfully, 'as if he came just to get a sight of us.'

'And he got it. Ah, providence is good to the poor.'

'Whoever's behind those tenements isn't going to stick at any odd trifle. We must watch out. That man was probably sent to mark us down for one of the gangs. Now they'll know what we look like, and they can get after us.'

'These are the drawbacks to being public men, Comrade Windsor. We must bear them manfully, without wincing.'

Billy turned again to his work.

'I'm not going to wince,' he said, 'so's you could notice it with a microscope. What I'm going to do is to buy a good big stick. And I'd advise you to do the same.'

It was by Psmith's suggestion that the editorial staff of *Cosy Moments* dined that night in the roof-garden at the top of the Astor Hotel.

'The tired brain,' he said, 'needs to recuperate. To feed on such a night as this in some low-down hostelry on the level of the street, with German waiters breathing heavily down the back of one's neck and two fiddles and a piano whacking out 'Beautiful Eyes' about three feet from one's tympanum, would be false economy. Here, fanned by cool breezes and surrounded by fair women and brave men, one may do a bit of tissue-restoring. Moreover, there is little danger up here of being slugged by our moth-eaten acquaintance of this morning. A man with trousers like his would not be allowed in. We shall probably find him waiting for us at the main entrance with a sand-bag, when we leave, but, till then – '

He turned with gentle grace to his soup.

It was a warm night, and the roof-garden was full. From where they sat they could see the million twinkling lights of the city. Towards the end of the meal, Psmith's gaze concentrated itself on the advertisement of a certain brand of ginger-ale in Times Square. It is a mass of electric light arranged in the shape of a great bottle, and at regular intervals there proceed from the bottle's mouth flashes of flame representing ginger-ale. The thing began to exercise a hypnotic effect on Psmith. He came to himself with a start, to find Billy Windsor in conversation with a waiter.

'Yes, my name's Windsor,' Billy was saying.

The waiter bowed and retired to one of the tables where a young man in evening clothes was seated. Psmith recollected having seen this solitary diner looking in their direction once or twice during dinner, but the fact had not impressed him.

'What is happening, Comrade Windsor?' he inquired. 'I was musing with a certain tenseness at the moment, and the rush of events has left me behind.'

'Man at that table wanted to know if my name was Windsor,' said Billy.

'Ah?' said Psmith, interested; 'and was it?'

'Here he comes. I wonder what he wants. I don't know the man from Adam.'

The stranger was threading his way between the tables.

'Can I have a word with you, Mr Windsor?' he said.

Billy looked at him curiously. Recent events had made him wary of strangers.

'Won't you sit down?' he said.

A waiter was bringing a chair. The young man seated himself.

'By the way,' added Billy; 'my friend, Mr Smith.'

'Pleased to meet you,' said the other.

'I don't know your – ' Billy hesitated.

'Never mind about my name,' said the stranger. 'It won't be needed. Is Mr Smith on your paper? Excuse my asking.'

Psmith bowed.

'That's all right, then. I can go ahead.'

He bent forward.

'Neither of you gentlemen are hard of hearing, eh?'

'In the old prairie days.' said Psmith. 'Comrade Windsor was known to the Indians as Boola-Ba-Na-Gosh, which, as you doubtless know, signifies Big-Chief-Who-Can-Hear-A-Fly-Clear-Its-Throat. I too can hear as well as the next man. Why?'

'That's all right, then. I don't want to have to shout it. There's some things it's better not to yell.'

He turned to Billy, who had been looking at him all the while with a combination of interest and suspicion. The man might or might not be friendly. In the meantime, there was no harm in being on one's guard. Billy's experience as a cub-reporter had given him the knowledge that is only given in its entirety to police and newspaper men: that there are two New Yorks. One is a modern, well-policed city, through which one may walk from end to end without encountering adventure. The other is a city as full of sinister intrigue, of whisperings and conspiracies, of battle, murder, and sudden death in dark by-ways, as any town of medieval Italy. Given certain conditions, anything may happen to any one in New York. And Billy realized that these conditions now prevailed in his own case. He had come into conflict with New York's underworld. Circumstances had placed him below the surface, where only his wits could help him.

'It's about that tenement business,' said the stranger.

Billy bristled. 'Well, what about it?' he demanded truculently.

The stranger raised a long and curiously delicately shaped hand. 'Don't bite at me,' he said. 'This isn't my funeral. I've no kick coming. I'm a friend.'

'Yet you don't tell us your name.'

'Never mind my name. If you were in my line of business, you wouldn't be so durned stuck on this name thing. Call me Smith, if you like.'

'You could select no nobler pseudonym,' said Psmith cordially.

'Eh? Oh, I see. Well, make it Brown, then. Anything you please. It don't signify. See here, let's get back. About this tenement thing. You understand certain parties have got it against you?'

'A charming conversationalist, one Comrade Parker, hinted

64

at something of the sort,' said Psmith, 'in a recent interview. *Cosy Moments,* however, cannot be muzzled.'

'Well?' said Billy.

'You're up against a big proposition.'

'We can look after ourselves.'

'Gum! you'll need to. The man behind is a big bug.'

Billy leaned forward eagerly.

'Who is he?'

The other shrugged his shoulders.

'I don't know. You wouldn't expect a man like that to give himself away.'

'Then how do you know he's a big bug?'

'Precisely,' said Psmith. 'On what system have you estimated the size of the gentleman's bughood?'

The stranger lit a cigar.

'By the number of dollars he was ready to put up to have you done in.'

Billy's eyes snapped.

'Oh?' he said. 'And which gang has he given the job to?'

'I wish I could tell you. He – his agent, that is – came to Bat Jarvis.'

'The cat-expert?' said Psmith. 'A man of singularly winsome personality.'

'Bat turned the job down.'

'Why was that?' inquired Billy.

'He said he needed the money as much as the next man, but when he found out who he was supposed to lay for, he gave his job the frozen face. Said you were a friend of his and none of his fellows were going to put a finger on you. I don't know what you've been doing to Bat, but he's certainly Willie the Long-Lost Brother with you.'

'A powerful argument in favour of kindness to animals!' said Psmith. 'Comrade Windsor came into possession of one of Comrade Jarvis's celebrated stud of cats. What did he do? Instead of having the animal made into a nourishing soup, he restored it to its bereaved owner. Observe the sequel. He is now as a prize tortoiseshell to Comrade Jarvis.'

'So Bat wouldn't stand for it?' said Billy.

'Not on his life. Turned it down without a blink. And he sent me along to find you and tell you so.'

'We are much obliged to Comrade Jarvis,' said Psmith.

'He told me to tell you to watch out, because another gang is dead sure to take on the job. But he said you were to know he wasn't mixed up in it. He also said that any time you were in bad, he'd do his best for you. You've certainly made the biggest kind of hit with Bat. I haven't seen him so worked up over a thing in years. Well, that's all, I reckon. Guess I'll be pushing along. I've a date to keep. Glad to have met you. Glad to have met you, Mr Smith. Pardon me, you have an insect on your coat.'

He flicked at Psmith's coat with a quick movement. Psmith thanked him gravely.

'Good night,' concluded the stranger, moving off.

For a few moments after he had gone, Psmith and Billy sat smoking in silence. They had plenty to think about.

'How's the time going?' asked Billy at length.

Psmith felt for his watch, and looked at Billy with some sadness.

'I am sorry to say, Comrade Windsor – '

'Hullo,' said Billy, 'here's that man coming back again.'

The stranger came up to their table, wearing a light overcoat over his dress clothes. From the pocket of this he produced a gold watch.

'Force of habit,' he said apologetically, handing it to Psmith. 'You'll pardon me. Good night, gentlemen, again.'

12. A Red Taximeter

The Astor Hotel faces on to Times Square. A few paces to the right of the main entrance the Times Building towers to the sky; and at the foot of this the stream of traffic breaks, forming two channels. To the right of the building is Seventh Avenue, quiet, dark, and dull. To the left is Broadway, the Great White Way, the longest, straightest, brightest, wickedest street in the world.

Psmith and Billy, having left the Astor, started to walk down Broadway to Billy's lodgings in Fourteenth Street. The usual crowd was drifting slowly up and down in the glare of the white lights.

They had reached Herald Square, when a voice behind them exclaimed, 'Why, it's Mr Windsor.'

They wheeled round. A flashily dressed man was standing with outstretched hand.

'I saw you come out of the Astor,' he said cheerily. 'I said to myself, "I know that man." Darned if I could put a name to you, though. So I just followed you along, and right here it came to me.'

'It did, did it?' said Billy politely.

'It did, sir. I've never set eyes on you before, but I've seen so many photographs of you that I reckon we're old friends. I know your father very well, Mr Windsor. He showed me the photographs. You may have heard him speak of me – Jack Lake? How is the old man? Seen him lately?'

'Not for some time. He was well when he last wrote.'

'Good for him. He would be. Tough as a plank, old Joe Windsor. We always called him Joe.'

'You'd have known him down in Missouri, of course?' said Billy.

'That's right. In Missouri. We were side-partners for years. Now, see here, Mr Windsor, it's early yet. Won't you and your friend come along with me and have a smoke and a chat? I live right here in Thirty-Third Street. I'd be right glad for you to come.'

'I don't doubt it,' said Billy, 'but I'm afraid you'll have to excuse us.'

'In a hurry, are you?'

'Not in the least.'

'Then come right along.'

'No, thanks.'

'Say, why not? It's only a step.'

'Because we don't want to. Good night.'

He turned, and started to walk away. The other stood for a moment, staring; then crossed the road.

Psmith broke the silence.

'Correct me if I am wrong, Comrade Windsor,' he said tentatively, 'but were you not a trifle – shall we say abrupt? – with the old family friend?'

Billy Windsor laughed.

'If my father's name was Joseph,' he said, 'instead of being William, the same as mine, and if he'd ever been in Missouri in his life, which he hasn't, and if I'd been photographed since I was a kid, which I haven't been, I might have gone along. As it was, I thought it better not to.'

'These are deep waters, Comrade Windsor. Do you mean to intimate – ?'

'If they can't do any better than that, we shan't have much to worry us. What do they take us for, I wonder? Farmers? Playing off a comic-supplement bluff like that on us!'

There was honest indignation in Billy's voice.

'You think, then, that if we had accepted Comrade Lake's invitation, and gone along for a smoke and a chat, the chat would not have been of the pleasantest nature?'

'We should have been put out of business.'

'I have heard so much,' said Psmith, thoughtfully, 'of the lavish hospitality of the American.'

'Taxi, sir?'

A red taximeter cab was crawling down the road at their side. Billy shook his head.

'Not that a taxi would be an unsound scheme,' said Psmith.

'Not that particular one, if you don't mind.'

'Something about it that offends your aesthetic taste?' queried Psmith sympathetically.

'Something about it makes my aesthetic taste kick like a mule,' said Billy.

'Ah, we highly strung literary men do have these curious prejudices. We cannot help it. We are the slaves of our temperaments. Let us walk, then. After all, the night is fine, and we are young and strong.'

They had reached Twenty-Third Street when Billy stopped. 'I don't know about walking,' he said. 'Suppose we take the Elevated?'

'Anything you wish, Comrade Windsor. I am in your hands.'

They cut across into Sixth Avenue, and walked up the stairs to the station of the Elevated Railway. A train was just coming in.

'Has it escaped your notice, Comrade Windsor,' said Psmith after a pause. 'that, so far from speeding to your lodgings, we are going in precisely the opposite direction? We are in an up-town train.'

'I noticed it,' said Billy briefly.

'Are we going anywhere in particular?'

'This train goes as far as Hundred and Tenth Street. We'll go up to there.'

'And then?'

'And then we'll come back.'

'And after that, I suppose, we'll make a trip to Philadelphia, or Chicago, or somewhere? Well, well, I am in your hands, Comrade Windsor. The night is yet young. Take me where you will. It is only five cents a go, and we have money in our purses. We are two young men out for reckless dissipation. By all means let us have it.'

At Hundred and Tenth Street they left the train, went down the stairs, and crossed the street. Half-way across Billy stopped.

'What now, Comrade Windsor?' inquired Psmith patiently. 'Have you thought of some new form of entertainment?'

Billy was making for a spot some few yards down the road. Looking in that direction, Psmith saw his objective. In the shadow of the Elevated there was standing a taximeter cab.

'Taxi, sir?' said the driver, as they approached.

'We are giving you a great deal of trouble,' said Billy. 'You must be losing money over this job. All this while you might be getting fares down-town.'

'These meetings, however,' urged Psmith, 'are very pleasant.'

'I can save you worrying,' said Billy. 'My address is 84 East Fourteenth Street. We are going back there now.'

'Search me,' said the driver, 'I don't know what you're talking about.'

'I thought perhaps you did,' replied Billy. 'Good night.'

'These things are very disturbing,' said Psmith, when they were in the train. 'Dignity is impossible when one is compelled to be the Hunted Fawn. When did you begin to suspect that yonder merchant was doing the sleuth-hound act?'

'When I saw him in Broadway having a heart-to-heart talk with our friend from Missouri.'

'He must be something of an expert at the game to have kept on our track.'

'Not on your life. It's as easy as falling off a log. There are only certain places where you can get off an Elevated train. All he'd got to do was to get there before the train, and wait. I didn't expect to dodge him by taking the Elevated. I just wanted to make certain of his game.'

The train pulled up at the Fourteenth Street station. In the roadway at the foot of the opposite staircase was a red taximeter cab.

13. Reviewing the Situation

Arriving at the bed-sitting-room, Billy proceeded to occupy the rocking-chair, and, as was his wont, began to rock himself rhythmically to and fro. Psmith seated himself gracefully on the couch-bed. There was a silence.

The events of the evening had been a revelation to Psmith. He had not realized before the extent of the ramifications of New York's underworld. That members of the gangs should crop up in the Astor roof-garden and in gorgeous raiment in the middle of Broadway was a surprise. When Billy Windsor had mentioned the gangs, he had formed a mental picture of low-browed hooligans, keeping carefully to their own quarter of the town. This picture had been correct, as far as it went, but it had not gone far enough. The bulk of the gangs of New York are of the hooligan class, and are rarely met with outside their natural boundaries. But each gang has its more prosperous members; gentlemen, who, like the man of the Astor roof-garden, support life by more delicate and genteel methods than the rest. The main body rely for their incomes, except at election-time, on such primitive feats as robbing intoxicated pedestrians. The aristocracy of the gangs soar higher.

It was a considerable time before Billy spoke.

'Say,' he said, 'this thing wants talking over.'

'By all means, Comrade Windsor.'

'It's this way. There's no doubt now that we're up against a mighty big proposition.'

'Something of the sort would seem to be the case.'

'It's like this. I'm going to see this through. It isn't only that I want to do a bit of good to the poor cusses in those tenements, though I'd do it for that alone. But, as far as I'm concerned, there's something to it besides that. If we win out, I'm going to get a job out of one of the big dailies. It'll give me just the chance I need. See what I mean? Well, it's different with you. I don't see that it's up to you to run the risk of getting yourself put out of business with a blackjack, and maybe shot. Once you get mixed up with the gangs there's no saying what's going to be doing. Well, I don't see why you shouldn't quit. All this has got nothing to do with you. You're over here on a vacation. You haven't got to make a living this side. You want to go about and have a good time, instead of getting mixed up with – '

He broke off.

'Well, that's what I wanted to say, anyway,' he concluded.

Psmith looked at him reproachfully.

'Are you trying to *sack* me, Comrade Windsor?'

'How's that?'

'In various treatises on "How to Succeed in Literature",' said Psmith sadly, 'which I have read from time to time, I have always found it stated that what the novice chiefly needed was an editor who believed in him. In you, Comrade Windsor, I fancied that I had found such an editor.'

'What's all this about?' demanded Billy. 'I'm making no kick about your work.'

'I gathered from your remarks that you were anxious to receive my resignation.'

'Well, I told you why. I didn't want you to be black-jacked.'

'Was that the only reason?'

'Sure.'

'Then all is well,' said Psmith, relieved. 'For the moment I fancied that my literary talents had been weighed in the balance and adjudged below par. If that is all – why, these are the mere everyday risks of the young journalist's life. Without them we should be dull and dissatisfied. Our work would lose its fire. Men such as ourselves, Comrade Windsor, need a certain stimulus, a certain fillip, if they are to keep up their high standards. The knowledge that a low-browed gentleman is waiting round the corner with a sand-bag poised in air will just supply that stimulus. Also that fillip. It will give our output precisely the edge it requires.'

Then you'll stay in this thing? You'll stick to the work?'

'Like a conscientious leech, Comrade Windsor.'

'Bully for you,' said Billy.

It was not Psmith's habit, when he felt deeply on any subject, to exhibit his feelings; and this matter of the tenements had hit him harder than any one who did not know him intimately would have imagined. Mike would have understood him, but Billy Windsor was too recent an acquaintance. Psmith was one of those people who are content to accept most of the happenings of life in an airy spirit of tolerance. Life had been more or less of a game with him up till now. In his previous encounters with those with whom fate had brought him in contact there had been little at stake. The prize of victory had been merely a comfortable feeling of having had the best of a battle of wits; the penalty of defeat nothing worse than the discomfort of having failed to score. But this tenement business was different Here he had touched the realities. There was something worth fighting for. His lot had been cast in pleasant places, and the sight of actual raw misery had come home to him with an added force from that circumstance. He was fully aware of the risks that he must run. The words of the man at the Astor, and still more the episodes of the family friend from Missouri and the taximeter cab, had shown him that this thing was on a different plane from anything that had happened to him before. It was a fight without the gloves, and to a finish at that. But he meant to see it through. Somehow or other those tenement houses had got to be cleaned up. If it meant trouble, as it undoubtedly did, that trouble would have to be faced.

'Now that Comrade Jarvis,' he said, 'showing a spirit of forbearance which, I am bound to say, does him credit, has declined the congenial task of fracturing our occiputs, who should you say, Comrade Windsor, would be the chosen substitute?'

Billy shook his head. 'Now that Bat has turned up the job, it might be any one of three gangs. There are four main gangs, you know. Bat's is the biggest. But the smallest of them's large enough to put us away, if we give them the chance.'

'I don't quite grasp the nice points of this matter. Do you

mean that we have an entire gang on our trail in one solid mass, or will it be merely a section?'

'Well, a section, I guess, if it comes to that. Parker, or whoever fixed this thing up, would go to the main boss of the gang. If it was the Three Points, he'd go to Spider Reilly. If it was the Table Hill lot, he'd look up Dude Dawson. And so on.'

'And what then?'

'And then the boss would talk it over with his own special partners. Every gang-leader has about a dozen of them. A sort of Inner Circle. They'd fix it up among themselves. The rest of the gang wouldn't know anything about it. The fewer in the game, you see, the fewer to split up the dollars.'

'I see. Then things are not so black. All we have to do is to look out for about a dozen hooligans with a natural dignity in their bearing, the result of intimacy with the main boss. Carefully eluding these aristocrats, we shall win through. I fancy, Comrade Windsor, that all may yet be well. What steps do you propose to take by way of self-defence?'

'Keep out of the middle of the street, and not go off the Broadway after dark. You're pretty safe on Broadway. There's too much light for them there.'

'Now that our sleuth-hound friend in the taximeter has ascertained your address, shall you change it?'

'It wouldn't do any good. They'd soon find where I'd gone to. How about yours?'

'I fancy I shall be tolerably all right. A particularly massive policeman is on duty at my very doors. So much for our private lives. But what of the day-time? Suppose these sand-bag-specialists drop in at the office during business hours. Will Comrade Maloney's frank and manly statement that we are not in be sufficient to keep them out? I doubt it. All unused to the nice conventions of polite society, these rugged persons will charge through. In such circumstances good work will be hard to achieve. Your literary man must have complete quiet if he is to give the public of his best. But stay. An idea!'

'Well?'

'Comrade Brady. The Peerless Kid. The man *Cosy Moments* is running for the light-weight championship. We are his pugilistic sponsors. You may say that it is entirely owing to our efforts that he has obtained this match with – who exactly is the gentleman Comrade Brady fights at the Highfield Club on Friday night?'

'Cyclone Al. Wolmann, isn't it?'

'You are right. As I was saying, but for us the privilege of smiting Comrade Cyclone Al. Wolmann under the fifth rib on Friday night would almost certainly have been denied to him.'

It almost seemed as if he were right. From the moment the paper had taken up his cause, Kid Brady's star had undoubtedly been in the ascendant. People began to talk about him as a likely man. Edgren, in the *Evening World,* had a paragraph about his chances for the light-weight title. Tad, in the *Journal,* drew a picture of him. Finally, the management of the Highfield Club had signed him for a ten-round bout with Mr Wolmann. There were, therefore, reasons why *Cosy Moments* should feel a claim on the Kid's services.

'He should,' continued Psmith, 'if equipped in any degree with finer feelings, be bubbling over with gratitude towards us. "But for *Cosy Moments*," he should be saying to himself, "where should I be? Among the also-rans." I imagine that he will do any little thing we care to ask of him. I suggest that we approach Comrade Brady, explain the facts of the case, and offer him at a comfortable salary the post of fighting-editor of *Cosy Moments*. His duties will be to sit in the room opening out of ours, girded as to the loins and full of martial spirit, and apply some of those half-scissor hooks of his to the persons of any who overcome the opposition of Comrade Maloney. We, meanwhile, will enjoy the leisure and freedom from interruption which is so essential to the artist.'

'It's not a bad idea,' said Billy.

'It is about the soundest idea,' said Psmith, 'that has ever been struck. One of your newspaper friends shall supply us with tickets, and Friday night shall see us at the Highfield.'

14. The Highfield

Far up at the other end of the island, on the banks of the Harlem River, there stands the old warehouse which modern progress has converted into the Highfield Athletic and Gymnastic Club. The imagination, stimulated by the title, conjures up a sort of National Sporting Club, with pictures on the walls, padding on the chairs, and a sea of white shirt-fronts from roof to floor. But the Highfield differs in some respects from this fancy picture. Indeed, it would be hard to find a respect in which it does not differ. But these names are so misleading. The title under which the Highfield used to be known till a few years back was 'Swifty Bob's'. It was a good, honest title. You knew what to expect; and if you attended *séances* at Swifty Bob's you left your gold watch and your little savings at home. But a wave of anti-pugilistic feeling swept over the New York authorities. Promoters of boxing contests found themselves, to their acute disgust, raided by the police. The industry began to languish. People avoided places where at any moment the festivities might be marred by an inrush of large men in blue uniforms armed with locust-sticks.

And then some big-brained person suggested the club idea, which stands alone as an example of American dry humour. There are now no boxing contests in New York. Swifty Bob and his fellows would be shocked at the idea of such a thing. All that happens now is exhibition sparring bouts between members of the club. It is true that next day the papers very tactlessly report the friendly exhibition spar as if it had been quite a serious affair, but that is not the fault of Swifty Bob.

Kid Brady, the chosen of *Cosy Moments*, was billed for a 'ten-round exhibition contest', to be the main event of the evening's entertainment. No decisions are permitted at these clubs. Unless a regrettable accident occurs, and one of the sparrers is knocked out, the verdict is left to the newspapers next day. It is not uncommon to find a man win easily in the *World,* drawn in the *American,* and be badly beaten in the *Evening Mail.* The system leads to a certain amount of confusion, but it has the merit of offering consolation to a much-smitten warrior.

The best method of getting to the Highfield is by the Subway. To see the Subway in its most characteristic mood one must travel on it during the rush-hour, when its patrons are packed into the carriages in one solid jam by muscular guards and policemen, shoving in a manner reminiscent of a Rugby football scrum. When Psmith and Billy entered it on the Friday evening, it was comparatively empty. All the seats were occupied, but only a few of the straps and hardly any of the space reserved by law for the conductor alone.

Conversation on the Subway is impossible. The ingenious gentlemen who constructed it started with the object of making it noisy. Not ordinarily noisy, like a ton of coal falling on to a sheet of tin, but really noisy. So they fashioned the pillars of thin steel, and the sleepers of thin wood, and loosened all the nuts, and now a Subway train in motion suggests a prolonged dynamite explosion blended with the voice of some great cataract.

Psmith, forced into temporary silence by this combination of noises, started to make up for lost time on arriving in the street once more.

'A thoroughly unpleasant neighbourhood,' he said, critically surveying the dark streets. 'I fear me, Comrade Windsor, that we have been somewhat rash in venturing as far into the middle west as this. If ever there was a blighted locality where low-browed desperadoes might be expected to spring with whoops of joy from every corner, this blighted locality is that blighted locality. But we must carry on. In which direction, should you say, does this arena lie?'

It had begun to rain as they left Billy's lodgings. Psmith turned up the collar of his Burberry.

'We suffer much in the cause of Literature,' he said. 'Let us inquire of this genial soul if he knows where the Highfield is.'

The pedestrian referred to proved to be going there himself. They went on together, Psmith courteously offering views on the weather and forecasts of the success of Kid Brady in the approaching contest.

Rattling on, he was alluding to the prominent part *Cosy Moments* had played in the affair, when a rough thrust from Windsor's elbow brought home to him his indiscretion.

He stopped suddenly, wishing he had not said as much. Their connexion with that militant journal was not a thing even to be suggested to casual acquaintances, especially in such a particularly ill-lighted neighbourhood as that through which they were now passing.

Their companion, however, who seemed to be a man of small speech, made no comment. Psmith deftly turned the conversation back to the subject of the weather, and was deep in comparison of the respective climates of England and the United States, when they turned a corner and found themselves opposite a gloomy, barn-like building, over the door of which it was just possible to decipher in the darkness the words 'Highfield Athletic and Gymnastic Club'.

The tickets which Billy Windsor had obtained from his newspaper friend were for one of the boxes. These proved to be sort of sheep-pens of unpolished wood, each with four hard chairs in it. The interior of the Highfield Athletic and Gymnastic Club was severely free from anything in the shape of luxury and ornament. Along the four walls were raised benches in tiers. On these were seated as tough-looking a collection of citizens as one might wish to see. On chairs at the ring-side were the reporters, with tickers at their sides, by means of which they tapped details of each round through to their down-town offices, where write-up reporters were waiting to read off and elaborate the messages. In the centre of the room, brilliantly lighted by half a dozen electric chandeliers, was the ring.

There were preliminary bouts before the main event. A burly gentleman in shirt-sleeves entered the ring, followed by two slim youths in fighting costume and a massive person in a red jersey, blue serge trousers, and yellow braces, who chewed gum with an abstracted air throughout the proceedings.

The burly gentleman gave tongue in a voice that cleft the air like a cannon-ball.

'Ex-hib-it-i-on four-round bout between Patsy Milligan and Tommy Goodley, members of this club. Patsy on my right, Tommy on my left. Gentlemen will kindly stop smokin'.'

The audience did nothing of the sort. Possibly they did not apply the description to themselves. Possibly they considered the appeal a mere formula. Somewhere in the background a gong sounded, and Patsy, from the right, stepped briskly forward to meet Tommy, approaching from the left.

The contest was short but energetic. At intervals the combatants would cling affectionately to one another, and on these occasions the red-jerseyed man, still chewing gum and still wearing the same air of being lost in abstract thought, would split up the mass by the simple method of ploughing his way between the pair. Towards the end of the first round Thomas, eluding a left swing, put Patrick neatly to the floor, where the latter remained for the necessary ten seconds.

The remaining preliminaries proved disappointing. So much so that in the last of the series a soured sportsman on one of the benches near the roof began in satirical mood to whistle the 'Merry Widow Waltz'. It was here that the red-jerseyed thinker for the first and last time came out of his meditative trance. He leaned over the ropes, and spoke – without heat, but firmly.

'If that guy whistling back up yonder thinks he can do better than these boys, he can come right down into the ring.'

The whistling ceased.

There was a distinct air of relief when the last preliminary was finished and preparations for the main bout began. It did not commence at once. There were formalities to be gone through, introductions and the like. The burly gentleman reappeared from nowhere, ushering into the ring a sheepishly-grinning youth in flannel suit.

'In-ter-*doo*-cin' Young Leary,' he bellowed impressively, 'a noo member of this club, who will box some good boy here in September.'

He walked to the other side of the ring and repeated the remark. A raucous welcome was accorded to the new member.

Two other notable performers were introduced in a similar manner, and then the building became suddenly full of noise, for a tall youth in a bath-robe, attended by a little army of assistants, had entered the ring. One of the army carried a bright green bucket, on which were painted in white letters the words 'Cyclone Al. Wolmann'. A moment later there was another, though far lesser, uproar, as Kid Brady, his pleasant face wearing a self-confident smirk, ducked under the ropes and sat down in the opposite corner.

'Ex-hib-it-i-on ten-round bout,' thundered the burly gentle-man, 'between Cyclone Al. Wolmann – '

Loud applause. Mr Wolmann was one of the famous, a fighter with a reputation from New York to San Francisco. He was generally considered the most likely man to give the hitherto invincible Jimmy Garvin a hard battle for the light-weight championship.

'Oh, you Al.!' roared the crowd.

Mr Wolmann bowed benevolently.

' – and Kid Brady, members of this – '

There was noticeably less applause for the Kid. He was an unknown. A few of those present had heard of his victories in the West, but these were but a small section of the crowd. When the faint applause had ceased, Psmith rose to his feet.

'Oh, you Kid!' he observed encouragingly. 'I should not like Comrade Brady,' he said, reseating himself, 'to think that he has no friend but his poor old mother, as, you will recollect, occurred on a previous occasion.'

The burly gentleman, followed by the two armies of assistants, dropped down from the ring, and the gong sounded.

Mr Wolmann sprang from his corner as if somebody had touched a spring. He seemed to be of the opinion that if you are a cyclone, it is never too soon to begin behaving like one. He danced round the Kid with an india-rubber agility. The *Cosy Moments* representative exhibited more stolidity. Except for the fact that he was in fighting attitude, with one gloved hand moving slowly in the neighbourhood of his stocky chest, and the other pawing the air on a line with his square jaw, one would have said that he did not realize the position of affairs. He wore the friendly smile of the good-natured guest who is led forward by his hostess to join in some round game.

Suddenly his opponent's long left shot out. The Kid, who had been strolling forward, received it under the chin, and continued to stroll forward as if nothing of note had happened. He gave the impression of being aware that Mr Wolmann had committed a breach of good taste and of being resolved to pass it off with ready tact.

The Cyclone, having executed a backward leap, a forward leap, and a feint, landed heavily with both hands. The Kid's genial smile did not even quiver, but he continued to move forward. His opponent's left flashed out again, but this time, instead of ignoring the matter, the Kid replied with a heavy right swing; and Mr Wolmann, leaping back, found himself against the ropes. By the time he had got out of that uncongenial position, two more of the Kid's swings had found their mark. Mr Wolmann, somewhat perturbed, scuttered out into the middle of the ring, the Kid following in his self-contained, solid way.

The Cyclone now became still more cyclonic. He had a left arm which seemed to open out in joints like a telescope. Several times when the Kid appeared well out of distance there was a thud as a brown glove ripped in over his guard and jerked his head back. But always he kept boring in, delivering an occasional right to the body with the pleased smile of an infant destroying a Noah's Ark with a tack-hammer. Despite these efforts, however, he was plainly getting all the worst of it. Energetic Mr Wolmann, relying on his long left, was putting in three blows to his one. When the gong sounded, ending the first round, the house was practically solid for the Cyclone. Whoops and yells rose from everywhere. The building rang with shouts of, 'Oh, you Al!'

Psmith turned sadly to Billy.

'It seems to me, Comrade Windsor,' he said, 'that this merry meeting looks like doing Comrade Brady no good. I should not be surprised at any moment to see his head bounce off on to the floor.'

'Wait,' said Billy. 'He'll win yet.'

'You think so?'

'Sure. He comes from Wyoming,' said Billy with simple confidence.

Rounds two and three were a repetition of round one. The Cyclone raged almost unchecked about the ring. In one lightning rally in the third he brought his right across squarely on to the Kid's jaw. It was a blow which should have knocked any boxer out. The Kid merely staggered slightly and returned to business, still smiling.

'See!' roared Billy enthusiastically in Psmith's ear, above the uproar. 'He doesn't mind it! He likes it! He comes from Wyoming!'

With the opening of round four there came a subtle change. The Cyclone's fury was expending itself. That long left shot out less sharply. Instead of being knocked back by it, the *Cosy Moments* champion now took the hits in his stride, and came shuffling in with his damaging body-blows. There were cheers and 'Oh, you Al.'s!' at the sound of the gong, but there was an appealing note in them this time. The gallant sportsmen whose connexion with boxing was confined to watching other men fight, and betting on what they considered a certainty, and who would have expired promptly if any one had tapped them sharply on their well-filled waistcoats, were beginning to fear that they might lose their money after all.

In the fifth round the thing became a certainty. Like the month of March, the Cyclone, who had come in like a lion, was going out like a lamb. A slight decrease in the pleasantness of the Kid's smile was noticeable. His expression began to resemble more nearly the gloomy importance of the *Cosy Moments* photographs. Yells of agony from panic-stricken speculators around the ring began to smite the rafters. The Cyclone, now but a gentle breeze, clutched repeatedly, hanging on like a leech till removed by the red-jerseyed referee.

Suddenly a grisly silence fell upon the house. It was broken by a cowboy yell from Billy Windsor. For the Kid, battered, but obviously content, was standing in the middle of the ring, while on the ropes the Cyclone, drooping like a wet sock, was sliding slowly to the floor.

'*Cosy Moments* wins,' said Psmith. 'An omen, I fancy, Comrade Windsor.'

15. An Addition to the Staff

Penetrating into the Kid's dressing-room some moments later, the editorial staff found the winner of the ten-round exhibition bout between members of the club seated on a chair, having his right leg rubbed by a shock-headed man in a sweater, who had been one of his seconds during the conflict. The Kid beamed as they entered.

'Gents,' he said, 'come right in. Mighty glad to see you.'

'It is a relief to me, Comrade Brady,' said Psmith, 'to find that you *can* see us. I had expected to find that Comrade Wolmann's purposeful biffs had completely closed your star-likes.'

'Sure, I never felt them. He's a good quick boy, is Al., but,' continued the Kid with powerful imagery, 'he couldn't hit a hole in a block of ice-cream, not if he was to use a hammer.'

'And yet at one period in the proceedings, Comrade Brady,' said Psmith, 'I fancied that your head would come unglued at the neck. But the fear was merely transient. When you began to administer those – am I correct in saying? – half-scissor hooks to the body, why, then I felt like some watcher of the skies when a new planet swims into his ken; or like stout Cortez when with eagle eyes he stared at the Pacific.'

The Kid blinked.

'How's that?' he inquired.

'And why did I feel like that, Comrade Brady? I will tell you. Because my faith in you was justified. Because there before me stood the ideal fighting-editor of *Cosy Moments*. It is not a post that any weakling can fill. There charm of manner cannot qualify a man for the position. No one can hold down the job simply by having a kind heart or being good at farmyard imitations. No. We want a man of thews and sinews, a man who would rather be hit on the head with a half-brick than not. And you, Comrade Brady, are such a man.'

The Kid turned appealingly to Billy.

'Say, this gets past me, Mr Windsor. Put me wise.'

'Can we have a couple of words with you alone, Kid?' said Billy. 'We want to talk over something with you.'

'Sure. Sit down, gents. Jack'll be through in a minute.'

Jack, who during this conversation had been concentrating himself on his subject's left leg, now announced that he guessed that would about do, and having advised the Kid not to stop and pick daisies, but to get into his clothes at once before he caught a chill, bade the company good night and retired.

Billy shut the door.

'Kid,' he said, 'you know those articles about the tenements we've been having in the paper?'

'Sure. I read 'em. They're to the good.'

Psmith bowed.

'You stimulate us, Comrade Brady. This is praise from Sir Hubert Stanley.'

'It was about time some strong josher came and put it across to 'em,' added the Kid.

'So we thought. Comrade Parker, however, totally disagreed with us.'

'Parker?'

'That's what I'm coming to,' said Billy. 'The day before yesterday a man named Parker called at the office and tried to buy us off.'

Billy's voice grew indignant at the recollection.

'You gave him the hook, I guess?' queried the interested Kid.

'To such an extent, Comrade Brady,' said Psmith, 'that he left breathing threatenings and slaughter. And it is for that reason that we have ventured to call upon you.'

'It's this way,' said Billy. 'We're pretty sure by this time that whoever the man is this fellow Parker's working for has put one of the gangs on to us.'

'You don't say!' exclaimed the Kid. 'Gum! Mr Windsor, they're tough propositions, those gangs.'

'We've been followed in the streets, and once they put up a bluff to get us where they could do us in. So we've come along to you. We can look after ourselves out of the office, you see, but what we want is some one to help in case they try to rush us there.'

'In brief, a fighting-editor,' said Psmith. 'At all costs we must have privacy. No writer can prune and polish his sentences to his satisfaction if he is compelled constantly to break off in order to eject boisterous hooligans. We therefore offer you the job of sitting in the outer room and intercepting these bravoes before they can reach us. The salary we leave to you. There are doubloons and to spare in the old oak chest. Take what you need and put the rest – if any – back. How does the offer strike you. Comrade Brady?'

'We don't want to get you in under false pretences, Kid,' said Billy. 'Of course, they may not come anywhere near the office. But still, if they did, there would be something doing. What do you feel about it?'

'Gents,' said the Kid, 'it's this way.'

He stepped into his coat, and resumed.

'Now that I've made good by getting the decision over Al., they'll be giving me a chance of a big fight. Maybe with Jimmy Garvin. Well, if that happens, see what I mean? I'll have to be going away somewhere and getting into training. I shouldn't be able to come and sit with you. But, if you gents feel like it, I'd be mighty glad to come in till I'm wanted to go into training-camp.'

'Great,' said Billy; 'that would suit us all the way up. If you'd do that, Kid, we'd be tickled to death.'

'And touching salary – ' put in Psmith.

'Shucks!' said the Kid with emphasis. 'Nix on the salary thing. I wouldn't take a dime. If it hadn't a-been for you gents, I'd have been waiting still for a chance of lining up in the championship class. That's good enough for me. Any old thing you gents want me to do, I'll do it. And glad, too.'

'Comrade Brady,' said Psmith warmly, 'you are, if I may say so, the goods. You are, beyond a doubt, supremely the stuff. We three, then, hand-in-hand, will face the foe; and if the foe has good, sound sense, he will keep right away. You appear to be ready. Shall we meander forth?'

The building was empty and the lights were out when they emerged from the dressing-room. They had to grope their way in darkness. It was still raining when they reached the street, and the only signs of life were a moist policeman and the distant glare of public-house lights down the road.

They turned off to the left, and, after walking some hundred yards, found themselves in a blind alley.

'Hullo!' said Billy. 'Where have we come to?'

Psmith sighed.

'In my trusting way,' he said, 'I had imagined that either you or Comrade Brady was in charge of this expedition and taking me by a known route to the nearest Subway station. I did not think to ask. I placed myself, without hesitation, wholly in your hands.'

'I thought the Kid knew the way,' said Billy.

'I was just taggin' along with you gents,' protested the light-weight, 'I thought you was taking me right. This is the first time I been up here.'

'Next time we three go on a little jaunt anywhere,' said Psmith resignedly, 'it would be as well to take a map and a corps of guides with us. Otherwise we shall start from Broadway and finish up at Minneapolis.'

They emerged from the blind alley and stood in the dark street, looking doubtfully up and down it.

'Aha!' said Psmith suddenly, 'I perceive a native. Several natives, in fact. Quite a little covey of them. We will put our case before them, concealing nothing, and rely on their advice to take us to our goal.'

A little knot of men was approaching from the left. In the darkness it was impossible to say how many of them there were. Psmith stepped forward, the Kid at his side.

'Excuse me, sir,' he said to the leader, 'but if you can spare me a moment of your valuable time –'

There was a sudden shuffle of feet on the pavement, a quick movement on the part of the Kid, a chunky sound as of wood striking wood, and the man Psmith had been addressing fell to the ground in a heap.

As he fell, something dropped from his hand on to the pavement with a bump and a rattle. Stooping swiftly, the Kid picked it up, and handed it to Psmith. His fingers closed upon it. It was a short, wicked-looking little bludgeon, the black-jack of the New York tough.

'Get busy,' advised the Kid briefly.

16. The First Battle

The promptitude and despatch with which the Kid had attended to the gentleman with the black-jack had not been without its effect on the followers of the stricken one. Physical courage is not an outstanding quality of the New York hooligan. His personal preference is for retreat when it is a question of unpleasantness with a stranger. And, in any case, even when warring among themselves, the gangs exhibit a lively distaste for the hard knocks of hand-to-hand fighting. Their chosen method of battling is to lie down on the ground and shoot. This is more suited to their physique, which is rarely great. The man, as a rule, is stunted and slight of build.

The Kid's rapid work on the present occasion created a good deal of confusion. There was no doubt that much had been hoped for from speedy attack. Also, the generalship of the expedition had been in the hands of the fallen warrior. His removal from the sphere of active influence had left the party without a head. And, to add to their discomfiture, they could not account for the Kid. Psmith they knew, and Billy Windsor they knew, but who was this stranger with the square shoulders and the upper-cut that landed like a cannon-ball? Something approaching a panic prevailed among the gang.

It was not lessened by the behaviour of the intended victims. Billy Windsor, armed with the big stick which he had bought after the visit of Mr Parker, was the first to join issue. He had been a few paces behind the others during the black-jack incident; but, dark as it was, he had seen enough to show him that the occasion was, as Psmith would have said, one for the Shrewd Blow rather than the Prolonged Parley. With a whoop of the purest Wyoming brand, he sprang forward into the confused mass of the enemy. A moment later Psmith and the Kid followed, and there raged over the body of the fallen leader a battle of Homeric type.

It was not a long affair. The rules and conditions governing the encounter offended the delicate sensibilities of the gang. Like artists who feel themselves trammelled by distasteful conventions, they were damped and could not do themselves justice. Their forte was long-range fighting with pistols. With that they felt *en rapport*. But this vulgar brawling in the darkness with muscular opponents who hit hard and often with sticks and hands was distasteful to them. They could not develop any enthusiasm for it. They carried pistols, but it was too dark and the combatants were too entangled to allow them to use these. Besides, this was not the dear, homely old Bowery, where a gentleman may fire a pistol without exciting vulgar comment. It was up-town, where curious crowds might collect at the first shot.

There was but one thing to be done. Reluctant as they might be to abandon their fallen leader, they must tear themselves away. Already they were suffering grievously from the stick, the black-jack, and the lightning blows of the Kid. For a moment they hung, wavering; then stampeded in half a dozen different directions, melting into the night whence they had come.

Billy, full of zeal, pursued one fugitive some fifty yards down the street, but his quarry, exhibiting a rare turn of speed, easily outstripped him.

He came back, panting, to find Psmith and the Kid examining the fallen leader of the departed ones with the aid of a match, which went out just as Billy arrived.

'It is our friend of the earlier part of the evening, Comrade Windsor,' said Psmith. 'The merchant with whom we hobnobbed on our way to the Highfield. In a moment of imprudence I mentioned *Cosy Moments*. I fancy that this was his first intimation that we were in the offing. His visit to the Highfield was paid, I think, purely from sport-loving motives. He was not on our trail. He came merely to see if Comrade Brady was proficient with his hands. Subsequent events must have justified our fighting editor in his eyes. It seems to be a moot point whether he will ever recover consciousness.'

'Mighty good thing if he doesn't,' said Billy uncharitably.

'From one point of view, Comrade Windsor, yes. Such an event would undoubtedly be an excellent thing for the public good. But from our point of view, it would be as well if he were to sit up and take notice. We could ascertain from him who he is and which particular collection of horny-handeds he represents. Light another match, Comrade Brady.'

The Kid did so. The head of it fell off and dropped upon the up-turned face. The hooligan stirred, shook himself, sat up, and began to mutter something in a foggy voice.

'He's still woozy,' said the Kid.

'Still – what exactly, Comrade Brady?'

'In the air,' explained the Kid. 'Bats in the belfry. Dizzy. See what I mean? It's often like that when a feller puts one in with a bit of weight behind it just where that one landed. Gum! I remember when I fought Martin Kelly; I was only starting to learn the game then. Martin and me was mixing it good and hard all over the ring, when suddenly he puts over a stiff one right on the point. What do you think I done? Fall down and take the count? Not on your life. I just turns round and walks straight out of the ring to my dressing-room. Willie Harvey, who was seconding me, comes tearing in after me, and finds me getting into my clothes. "What's doing, Kid?" he asks. "I'm going fishin', Willie," I says. "It's a lovely day." "You've lost the fight," he says. "Fight?" says I. "What fight?" See what I mean? I hadn't a notion of what had happened. It was a half an hour and more before I could remember a thing.'

During this reminiscence, the man on the ground had contrived to clear his mind of the mistiness induced by the Kid's upper-cut. The first sign he showed of returning intelligence was a sudden dash for safety up the road. But he had not gone five yards when he sat down limply.

The Kid was inspired to further reminiscence. 'Guess he's feeling pretty poor,' he said. 'It's no good him trying to run for a while after he's put his chin in the way of a real live one. I remember when Joe Peterson put me out, way back when I was new to the game – it was the same year I fought Martin Kelly. He had an awful punch, had old Joe, and he put me down and out in the eighth round. After the fight they found me on the fire-escape outside my dressing-room. "Come in, Kid," says they. "It's all right, chaps," I says, "I'm dying." Like that. "It's all right, chaps, I'm dying." Same with this guy. See what I mean?'

They formed a group about the fallen black-jack expert.

'Pardon us,' said Psmith courteously, 'for breaking in upon your reverie; but, if you could spare us a moment of your valuable time, there are one or two things which we should like to know.'

'Sure thing,' agreed the Kid.

'In the first place,' continued Psmith, 'would it be betraying professional secrets if you told us which particular bevy of energetic sandbaggers it is to which you are attached?'

'Gent,' explained the Kid, 'wants to know what's your gang.'

The man on the ground muttered something that to Psmith and Billy was unintelligible.

'It would be a charity,' said the former, 'if some phil-anthropist would give this blighter elocution lessons. Can you interpret, Comrade Brady?'

'Says it's the Three Points,' said the Kid.

'The Three Points? Let me see, is that Dude Dawson, Com-rade Windsor, or the other gentleman?'

'It's Spider Reilly. Dude Dawson runs the Table Hill crowd.'

'Perhaps this *is* Spider Reilly?'

'Nope,' said the Kid. 'I know the Spider. This ain't him. This is some other mutt.'

'Which other mutt in particular?' asked Psmith. 'Try and find out, Comrade Brady. You seem to be able to understand what he says. To me, personally, his remarks sound like the output of a gramophone with a hot potato in its mouth.'

'Says he's Jack Repetto,' announced the interpreter.

There was another interruption at this moment. The bashful Mr Repetto, plainly a man who was not happy in the society of strangers, made another attempt to withdraw. Reaching out a pair of lean hands, he pulled the Kid's legs from under him with a swift jerk, and, wriggling to his feet, started off again down the road. Once more, however, desire outran performance. He got as far as the nearest street-lamp, but no farther. The giddiness seemed to overcome him again, for he grasped the lamp-post, and, sliding slowly to the ground, sat there motionless.

The Kid, whose fall had jolted and bruised him, was inclined to be wrathful and vindictive. He was the first of the three to reach the elusive Mr Repetto, and if that worthy had happened to be standing instead of sitting it might have gone hard with him. But the Kid was not the man to attack a fallen foe. He contented himself with brushing the dust off his person and addressing a richly abusive flow of remarks to Mr Repetto.

Under the rays of the lamp it was possible to discern more closely the features of the black-jack exponent. There was a subtle but noticeable resemblance to those of Mr Bat Jarvis. Apparently the latter's oiled forelock, worn low over the forehead, was more a concession to the general fashion prevailing in gang circles than an expression of personal taste. Mr Repetto had it, too. In his case it was almost white, for the fallen warrior was an albino. His eyes, which were closed, had white lashes and were set as near together as Nature had been able to manage without actually running them into one another. His under-lip protruded and drooped. Looking at him, one felt instinctively that no judging committee of a beauty contest would hesitate a moment before him.

It soon became apparent that the light of the lamp, though bestowing the doubtful privilege of a clearer view of Mr Repetto's face, held certain disadvantages. Scarcely had the staff of *Cosy Moments* reached the faint yellow pool of light, in the centre of which Mr Repetto reclined, than, with a suddenness which caused them to leap into the air, there sounded from the darkness down the road the *crack-crack-crack* of a revolver. Instantly from the opposite direction came other shots. Three bullets flicked grooves in the roadway almost at Billy's feet. The Kid gave a sudden howl. Psmith's hat, suddenly imbued with life, sprang into the air and vanished, whirling into the night.

The thought did not come to them consciously at the moment, there being little time to think, but it was evident as soon as, diving out of the circle of light into the sheltering darkness, they crouched down and waited for the next move, that a somewhat skilful ambush had been effected. The other members of the gang, who had fled with such remarkable speed, had by no means been eliminated altogether from the game. While the questioning of Mr Repetto had been in progress, they had crept back, unperceived except by Mr Repetto himself. It being too dark for successful shooting, it had become Mr Repetto's task to lure his captors into the light, which he had accomplished with considerable skill.

For some minutes the battle halted. There was dead silence. The circle of light was empty now. Mr Repetto had vanished. A tentative shot from nowhere ripped through the air close to where Psmith lay flattened on the pavement. And then the pavement began to vibrate and give out a curious resonant sound. To Psmith it conveyed nothing, but to the opposing army it meant much. They knew it for what it was. Somewhere – it might be near or far – a policeman had heard the shots, and was signalling for help to other policemen along the line by beating on the flagstones with his night-stick, the New York constable's substitute for the London police-whistle. The noise grew, filling the still air. From somewhere down the road sounded the ring of running feet.

'De cops!' cried a voice. 'Beat it!'

Next moment the night was full of clatter. The gang was 'beating it'.

Psmith rose to his feet and dusted his clothes ruefully. For the first time he realized the horrors of war. His hat had gone for ever. His trousers could never be the same again after their close acquaintance with the pavement.

The rescue party was coming up at the gallop.

The New York policeman may lack the quiet dignity of his London rival, but he is a hustler.

'What's doing?'

'Nothing now,' said the disgusted voice of Billy Windsor from the shadows. 'They've beaten it.'

The circle of lamplight became as if by mutual consent a general rendezvous. Three grey-clad policemen, tough, clean-shaven men with keen eyes and square jaws, stood there, revolver in one hand, night-stick in the other. Psmith, hatless and dusty, joined them. Billy Windsor and the Kid, the latter bleeding freely from his left ear, the lobe of which had been chipped by a bullet, were the last to arrive.

'What's bin the rough house?' inquired one of the policemen, mildly interested.

'Do you know a sportsman of the name of Repetto?' inquired Psmith.

'Jack Repetto? Sure.'

'He belongs to the Three Points,' said another intelligent officer, as one naming some fashionable club.

'When next you see him,' said Psmith, 'I should be obliged if you would use your authority to make him buy me a new hat. I could do with another pair of trousers, too; but I will not press the trousers. A new hat, is, however, essential. Mine has a six-inch hole in it.'

'Shot at you, did they?' said one of the policemen, as who should say, 'Dash the lads, they're always up to some of their larks.'

'Shot at us!' burst out the ruffled Kid. 'What do you think's bin happening? Think an aeroplane ran into my ear and took half of it off? Think the noise was somebody opening bottles of pop? Think those guys that sneaked off down the road was just training for a Marathon?'

'Comrade Brady,' said Psmith, 'touches the spot. He – '

'Say, are you Kid Brady?' inquired one of the officers. For the first time the constabulary had begun to display any real animation.

'Reckoned I'd seen you somewhere!' said another. 'You licked Cyclone Al. all right, Kid, I hear.'

'And who but a bone-head thought he wouldn't?' demanded the third warmly. 'He could whip a dozen Cyclone Al.'s in the same evening with his eyes shut.'

'He's the next champeen,' admitted the first speaker.

'If he puts it over Jimmy Garvin,' argued the second.

'Jimmy Garvin!' cried the third. 'He can whip twenty Jimmy Garvins with his feet tied. I tell you – '

'I am loath,' observed Psmith, 'to interrupt this very impressive brain-barbecue, but, trivial as it may seem to you, to me there is a certain interest in this other little matter of my ruined hat. I know that it may strike you as hypersensitive of us to protest against being riddled with bullets, but – '

'Well, what's bin doin'?' inquired the Force. It was a nuisance, this perpetual harping on trifles when the deep question of the light-weight Championship of the World was under discussion, but the sooner it was attended to, the sooner it would be over.

Billy Windsor undertook to explain.

'The Three Points laid for us,' he said. 'Jack Repetto was bossing the crowd. I don't know who the rest were. The Kid put one over on to Jack Repetto's chin, and we were asking him a few questions when the rest came back, and started into shooting. Then we got to cover quick, and you came up and they beat it.'

'That,' said Psmith, nodding, 'is a very fair *précis* of the evening's events. We should like you, if you will be so good, to corral this Comrade Repetto, and see that he buys me a new hat.'

'We'll round Jack up,' said one of the policemen indulgently.

'Do it nicely,' urged Psmith. 'Don't go hurting his feelings.'

The second policeman gave it as his opinion that Jack was getting too gay. The third policeman conceded this. Jack, he said, had shown signs for some time past of asking for it in the neck. It was an error on Jack's part, he gave his hearers to understand, to assume that the lid was completely off the great city of New York.

'Too blamed fresh he's gettin',' the trio agreed. They could not have been more disapproving if they had been prefects at Haileybury and Mr Repetto a first-termer who had been detected in the act of wearing his cap on the back of his head.

They seemed to think it was too bad of Jack.

'The wrath of the Law,' said Psmith, 'is very terrible. We will leave the matter, then, in your hands. In the meantime, we should be glad if you would direct us to the nearest Subway station. Just at the moment, the cheerful lights of the Great White Way are what I seem chiefly to need.'

17. Guerilla Warfare

Thus ended the opening engagement of the campaign, seemingly in a victory for the *Cosy Moments* army. Billy Windsor, however, shook his head.

'We've got mighty little out of it,' he said.

'The victory,' said Psmith, 'was not bloodless. Comrade Brady's ear, my hat – these are not slight casualties. On the other hand, surely we are one up? Surely we have gained ground? The elimination of Comrade Repetto from the scheme of things in itself is something. I know few men I would not rather meet in a lonely road than Comrade Repetto. He is one of Nature's sand-baggers. Probably the thing crept upon him slowly. He started, possibly, in a merely tentative way by slugging one of the family circle. His nurse, let us say, or his young brother. But, once started, he is unable to resist the craving. The thing grips him like dram-drinking. He sandbags now not because he really wants to, but because he cannot help himself. To me there is something singularly consoling in the thought that Comrade Repetto will no longer be among those present.'

'What makes you think that?'

'I should imagine that a benevolent Law will put him away in his little cell for at least a brief spell.'

'Not on your life,' said Billy. 'He'll prove an alibi.'

Psmith's eyeglass dropped out of his eye. He replaced it, and gazed, astonished, at Billy.

'An alibi? When three keen-eyed men actually caught him at it?'

'He can find thirty toughs to swear he was five miles away.'

'And get the court to believe it?' said Psmith.

'Sure,' said Billy disgustedly. 'You don't catch them hurting a gangsman unless they're pushed against the wall. The politicians don't want the gangs in gaol, especially as the Aldermanic elections will be on in a few weeks. Did you ever hear of Monk Eastman?'

'I fancy not, Comrade Windsor. If I did, the name has escaped me. Who was this cleric?'

'He was the first boss of the East Side gang, before Kid Twist took it on.'

'Yes?'

'He was arrested dozens of times, but he always got off. Do you know what he said once, when they pulled him for thugging a fellow out in New Jersey?'

'I fear not, Comrade Windsor. Tell me all.'

'He said, "You're arresting me, huh? Say, you want to look where you're goin'; I cut some ice in this town. I made half the big politicians in New York!" That was what he said.'

'His small-talk,' said Psmith, 'seems to have been bright and well-expressed. What happened then? Was he restored to his friends and his relations?'

'Sure, he was. What do you think? Well, Jack Repetto isn't Monk Eastman, but he's in with Spider Reilly, and the Spider's in with the men behind. Jack'll get off.'

'It looks to me, Comrade Windsor,' said Psmith thoughtfully, 'as if my stay in this great city were going to cost me a small fortune in hats.'

Billy's prophecy proved absolutely correct. The police were as good as their word. In due season they rounded up the impulsive Mr Repetto, and he was haled before a magistrate. And then, what a beautiful exhibition of brotherly love and auld-lang-syne camaraderie was witnessed! One by one, smirking sheepishly, but giving out their evidence with unshaken earnestness, eleven greasy, wandering-eyed youths mounted the witness-stand and affirmed on oath that at the time mentioned dear old Jack had been making merry in their company in a genial and law-abiding fashion, many, many blocks below the scene of the regrettable assault. The magistrate discharged the prisoner, and the prisoner, meeting Billy and Psmith in the street outside, leered triumphantly at them.

Billy stepped up to him. 'You may have wriggled out of this,' he said furiously, 'but if you don't get a move on and quit looking at me like that, I'll knock you over the Singer Building. Hump yourself.'

Mr Repetto humped himself.

So was victory turned into defeat, and Billy's jaw became squarer and his eye more full of the light of battle than ever. And there was need of a square jaw and a battlelit eye, for now began a period of guerilla warfare such as no New York paper had ever had to fight against.

It was Wheeler, the gaunt manager of the business side of the journal, who first brought it to the notice of the editorial staff. Wheeler was a man for whom in business hours nothing existed but his job; and his job was to look after the distribution of the paper. As to the contents of the paper he was absolutely ignorant. He had been with *Cosy Moments* from its start, but he had never read a line of it. He handled it as if it were so much soap. The scholarly writings of Mr Wilberfloss, the mirth-provoking sallies of Mr B. Henderson Asher, the tender outpourings of Luella Granville Waterman – all these were things outside his ken. He was a distributor, and he distributed.

A few days after the restoration of Mr Repetto to East Side Society, Mr Wheeler came into the editorial room with information and desire for information.

He endeavoured to satisfy the latter first.

'What's doing, anyway?' he asked. He then proceeded to his information. 'Someone's got it in against the paper, sure,' he said. 'I don't know what it's all about. I ha'n't never read the thing. Don't see what any one could have against a paper with a name like *Cosy Moments,* anyway. The way things have been going last few days, seems it might be the organ of a blamed mining-camp what the boys have took a dislike to.'

'What's been happening?' asked Billy with gleaming eyes.

'Why, nothing in the world to fuss about, only our carriers can't go out without being beaten up by gangs of toughs. Pat Harrigan's in the hospital now. Just been looking in on him. Pat's a feller who likes to fight. Rather fight he would than see a ball-game. But this was too much for him. Know what happened? Why, see here, just like this it was. Pat goes out with his cart. Passing through a low-down street on his way up-town he's held up by a bunch of toughs. He shows fight. Half a dozen of them attend to him, while the rest gets clean away with every copy of the paper there was in the cart. When the cop comes along, there's Pat in pieces on the ground and nobody in sight but a Dago chewing gum. Cop asks the Dago what's been doing, and the Dago says he's only just come round the corner and ha'n't seen nothing of anybody. What I want to know is, what's it all about? Who's got it in for us and why?'

Mr Wheeler leaned back in his chair, while Billy, his hair rumpled more than ever and his eyes glowing, explained the situation. Mr Wheeler listened absolutely unmoved, and, when the narrative had come to an end, gave it as his opinion that the editorial staff had sand. That was his sole comment.

'It's up to you,' he said, rising. 'You know your business. Say, though, someone had better get busy right quick and do something to stop these guys rough-housing like this. If we get a few more carriers beat up the way Pat was, there'll be a strike. It's not as if they were all Irishmen. The most of them are Dagoes and such, and they don't want any more fight than they can get by beating their wives and kicking kids off the sidewalk. I'll do my best to get this paper distributed right and it's a shame if it ain't, because it's going big just now – but it's up to you. Good day, gents.'

He went out. Psmith looked at Billy.

'As Comrade Wheeler remarks,' he said, 'it is up to us. What do you propose to do about it? This is a move of the enemy which I have not anticipated. I had fancied that their operations would be confined exclusively to our two selves. If they are going to strew the street with our carriers, we are somewhat in the soup.'

Billy said nothing. He was chewing the stem of an unlighted pipe. Psmith went on.

'It means, of course, that we must buck up to a certain extent. If the campaign is to be a long one, they have us where the hair is crisp. We cannot stand the strain. *Cosy Moments* cannot be muzzled, but it can undoubtedly be choked. What we want to do is to find out the name of the man behind the tenements as soon as ever we can and publish it; and, then, if we perish, fall yelling the name.'

Billy admitted the soundness of this scheme, but wished to know how it was to be done.

'Comrade Windsor,' said Psmith. 'I have been thinking this thing over, and it seems to me that we are on the wrong track, or rather we aren't on any track at all; we are simply marking time. What we want to do is to go out and hustle round till we stir up something. Our line up to the present has been to sit at home and scream vigorously in the hope of some stout fellow hearing and rushing to help. In other words, we've been saying in the paper what an out-size in scugs the merchant must be who owns those tenements, in the hope that somebody else will agree with us and be sufficiently interested to get to work and find out who the blighter is. That's all wrong. What we must do now, Comrade Windsor, is put on our hats, such hats as Comrade Repetto has left us, and sally forth as sleuth-hounds on our own account.'

'Yes, but how?' demanded Billy. 'That's all right in theory, but how's it going to work in practice? The only thing that can corner the man is a commission.'

'Far from it, Comrade Windsor. The job may be worked more simply. I don't know how often the rents are collected in these places, but I should say at a venture once a week. My idea is to hang negligently round till the rent-collector arrives, and when he has loomed upon the horizon, buttonhole him and ask him quite politely, as man to man, whether he is collecting those rents for himself or for somebody else, and if somebody else, who that somebody else is. Simple, I fancy? Yet brainy. Do you take me, Comrade Windsor?'

Billy sat up, excited. 'I believe you've hit it.'

Psmith shot his cuffs modestly.

18. An Episode by the Way

It was Pugsy Maloney who, on the following morning, brought to the office the gist of what is related in this chapter. Pugsy's version was, however, brief and unadorned, as was the way with his narratives. Such things as first causes and piquant details he avoided, as tending to prolong the telling excessively, thus keeping him from perusal of his cowboy stories. The way Pugsy put it was as follows. He gave the thing out merely as an item of general interest, a bubble on the surface of the life of a great city. He did not know how nearly interested were his employers in any matter touching that gang which is known as the Three Points. Pugsy said: 'Dere's trouble down where I live. Dude Dawson's mad at Spider Reilly, an' now de Table Hills are layin' for de T'ree Points. Sure.' He had then retired to his outer fastness, yielding further details jerkily and with the distrait air of one whose mind is elsewhere.

Skilfully extracted and pieced together, these details formed themselves into the following typical narrative of East Side life in New York.

The really important gangs of New York are four. There are other less important institutions, but these are little more than mere friendly gatherings of old boyhood chums for purposes of mutual companionship. In time they may grow, as did Bat Jarvis's coterie, into formidable organizations, for the soil is undoubtedly propitious to such growth. But at present the amount of ice which good judges declare them to cut is but small. They 'stick up' an occasional wayfarer for his 'cush', and they carry 'canisters' and sometimes fire them off, but these things do not signify the cutting of ice. In matters political there are only four gangs which count, the East Side, the Groome

Street, the Three Points, and the Table Hill. Greatest of these by virtue of their numbers are the East Side and the Groome Street, the latter presided over at the time of this story by Mr Bat Jarvis. These two are colossal, and, though they may fight each other, are immune from attack at the hands of lesser gangs. But between the other gangs, and especially between the Table Hill and the Three Points, which are much of a size, warfare rages as briskly as among the republics of South America. There has always been bad blood between the Table Hill and the Three Points, and until they wipe each other out after the manner of the Kilkenny cats, it is probable that there always will be. Little events, trifling in themselves, have always occurred to shatter friendly relations just when there has seemed a chance of their being formed. Thus, just as the Table Hillites were beginning to forgive the Three Points for shooting the redoubtable Paul Horgan down at Coney Island, a Three Pointer injudiciously wiped out another of the rival gang near Canal Street. He pleaded self-defence, and in any case it was probably mere thoughtlessness, but nevertheless the Table Hillites were ruffled.

That had been a month or so back. During that month things had been simmering down, and peace was just preparing to brood when there occurred the incident to which Pugsy had alluded, the regrettable falling out of Dude Dawson and Spider Reilly at Mr Maginnis's dancing saloon, Shamrock Hall, the same which Bat Jarvis had been called in to protect in the days before the Groome Street gang began to be.

Shamrock Hall, being under the eyes of the great Bat, was, of course, forbidden ground; and it was with no intention of spoiling the harmony of the evening that Mr Dawson had looked in. He was there in a purely private and peaceful character.

As he sat smoking, sipping, and observing the revels, there settled at the next table Mr Robert ('Nigger') Coston, an eminent member of the Three Points.

There being temporary peace between the two gangs, the great men exchanged a not unfriendly nod and, after a short pause, a word or two. Mr Coston, alluding to an Italian who had just pirouetted past, remarked that there sure was some class to the way that wop hit it up. Mr Dawson said Yup, there sure was. You would have said that all Nature smiled.

Alas! The next moment the sky was covered with black clouds and the storm broke. For Mr Dawson, continuing in this vein of criticism, rather injudiciously gave it as his opinion that one of the lady dancers had two left feet.

For a moment Mr Coston did not see which lady was alluded to.

'De goil in de pink skoit,' said Mr Dawson, facilitating the other's search by pointing with a much-chewed cigarette. It was at this moment that Nature's smile was shut off as if by a tap. For the lady in the pink skirt had been in receipt of Mr Coston's respectful devotion for the past eight days.

From this point onwards the march of events was rapid.

Mr Coston, rising, asked Mr Dawson who he thought he, Mr Dawson, was.

Mr Dawson, extinguishing his cigarette and placing it behind his ear, replied that he was the fellow who could bite his, Mr Coston's, head off.

Mr Coston said: 'Huh?'

Mr Dawson said: 'Sure.'

Mr Coston called Mr Dawson a pie-faced rubber-necked four-flusher.

Mr Dawson called Mr Coston a coon.

And that was where the trouble really started.

It was secretly a great grief to Mr Coston that his skin was of so swarthy a hue. To be permitted to address Mr Coston face to face by his nickname was a sign of the closest friendship, to which only Spider Reilly, Jack Repetto, and one or two more of the gang could aspire. Others spoke of him as Nigger, or, more briefly, Nig – strictly behind his back. For Mr Coston had a wide reputation as a fighter, and his particular mode of battling was to descend on his antagonist and bite him. Into this action he flung himself with the passionate abandonment of the artist. When he bit he bit. He did not nibble.

If a friend had called Mr Coston 'Nig' he would have been running grave risks. A stranger, and a leader of a rival gang, who addressed him as 'coon' was more than asking for trouble. He was pleading for it.

Great men seldom waste time. Mr Coston, leaning towards Mr Dawson, promptly bit him on the cheek. Mr Dawson bounded from his seat. Such was the excitement of the moment that, instead of drawing his 'canister', he forgot that he had one on his person, and, seizing a mug which had held beer, bounced it vigorously on Mr Coston's skull, which, being of solid wood, merely gave out a resonant note and remained unbroken.

So far the honours were comparatively even, with perhaps a slight balance in favour of Mr Coston. But now occurred an incident which turned the scale, and made war between the gangs inevitable. In the far corner of the room, surrounded by a crowd of admiring friends, sat Spider Reilly, monarch of the Three Points. He had noticed that there was a slight disturbance at the other side of the hall, but had given it little attention till, the dancing ceasing suddenly and the floor emptying itself of its crowd, he had a plain view of Mr Dawson and Mr Coston squaring up at each other for the second round. We must assume that Mr Reilly was not thinking what he did, for his action was contrary to all rules of gang-etiquette. In the street it would have been perfectly legitimate, even praiseworthy, but in a dance-hall belonging to a neutral power it was unpardonable.

What he did was to produce his 'canister' and pick off the unsuspecting Mr Dawson just as that exquisite was preparing to get in some more good work with the beer-mug. The leader of the Table Hillites fell with a crash, shot through the leg; and Spider Reilly, together with Mr Coston and others of the Three Points, sped through the doorway for safety, fearing the wrath of Bat Jarvis, who, it was known, would countenance no such episodes at the dance-hall which he had undertaken to protect.

Mr Dawson, meanwhile, was attended to and helped home. Willing informants gave him the name of his aggressor, and before morning the Table Hill camp was in ferment. Shooting broke out in three places, though there were no casualties. When the day dawned there existed between the two gangs a state of war more bitter than any in their record; for this time it was no question of obscure nonentities. Chieftain had assaulted chieftain; royal blood had been spilt.

'Comrade Windsor,' said Psmith, when Master Maloney had spoken his last word, 'we must take careful note of this little matter. I rather fancy that sooner or later we may be able to turn it to our profit. I am sorry for Dude Dawson, anyhow. Though I have never met him, I have a sort of instinctive respect for him. A man such as he would feel a bullet through his trouser-leg more than one of common clay who cared little how his clothes looked.'

19. In Pleasant Street

Careful inquiries, conducted incognito by Master Maloney among the denizens of Pleasant Street, brought the information that rents in the tenements were collected not weekly but monthly, a fact which must undoubtedly cause a troublesome hitch in the campaign. Rent-day, announced Pugsy, fell on the last day of the month.

'I rubbered around,' he said, 'and did de sleut' act, and I finds t'ings out. Dere's a feller comes round 'bout supper time dat day, an' den it's up to de fam'lies what lives in de tenements to dig down into deir jeans fer de stuff, or out dey goes dat same night.'

'Evidently a hustler, our nameless friend,' said Psmith.

'I got dat from a kid what knows anuder kid what lives dere,' explained Master Maloney. 'Say,' he proceeded confidentially, 'dat kid's in bad, sure he is. Dat second kid, de one what lives dere. He's a wop kid, an – '

'A what, Comrade Maloney?'

'A wop. A Dago. Why, don't you get next? Why, an Italian. Sure, dat's right. Well, dis kid, he is sure to be bad, 'cos his father come over from Italy to work on de Subway.'

'I don't see why that puts him in bad,' said Billy Windsor wonderingly.

'Nor I,' agreed Psmith. 'Your narratives, Comrade Maloney, always seem to me to suffer from a certain lack of construction. You start at the end, and then you go back to any portion of the story which happens to appeal to you at the moment, eventually winding up at the beginning. Why should the fact that this stripling's father has come over from Italy to work on the Subway be a misfortune?'

'Why, sure, because he got fired an' went an' swatted de

foreman one on de coco, an' de magistrate gives him t'oity days.'

'And then, Comrade Maloney? This thing is beginning to get clearer. You are like Sherlock Holmes. After you've explained a thing from start to finish – or, as you prefer to do, from finish to start – it becomes quite simple.'

'Why, den dis kid's in bad for fair, 'cos der ain't nobody to pungle de bones – '

'Pungle de what, Comrade Maloney?'

'De bones. De stuff. Dat's right. De dollars. He's all alone, dis kid, so when de rent-guy blows in, who's to slip him over de simoleons? It'll be outside for his, quick.'

Billy warmed up at this tale of distress in his usual way. 'Somebody ought to do something. It's a vile shame the kid being turned out like that.'

'We will see to it, Comrade Windsor. *Cosy Moments* shall step in. We will combine business with pleasure, paying the stripling's rent and corralling the rent-collector at the same time. What is today? How long before the end of the month? Another week! A murrain on it, Comrade Windsor. Two murrains. This delay may undo us.'

But the days went by without any further movement on the part of the enemy. A strange quiet seemed to be brooding over the other camp. As a matter of fact, the sudden outbreak of active hostilities with the Table Hill contingent had had the effect of taking the minds of Spider Reilly and his warriors off *Cosy Moments* and its affairs, much as the unexpected appearance of a mad bull would make a man forget that he had come out butterfly-hunting. Psmith and Billy could wait; they were not likely to take the offensive; but the Table Hillites demanded instant attention.

War had broken out, as was usual between the gangs, in a somewhat tentative fashion at first sight. There had been sniping and skirmishes by the wayside, but as yet no pitched battle. The two armies were sparring for an opening.

The end of the week arrived, and Psmith and Billy, conducted by Master Maloney, made their way to Pleasant Street.

To get there it was necessary to pass through a section of the enemy's country; but the perilous passage was safely negotiated. The expedition reached its unsavoury goal intact.

The wop kid, whose name, it appeared, was Giuseppe Orloni, inhabited a small room at the very top of the building next to the one Psmith and Mike had visited on their first appearance in Pleasant Street. He was out when the party, led by Pugsy up dark stairs, arrived; and, on returning, seemed both surprised and alarmed to see visitors. Pugsy undertook to do the honours. Pugsy as interpreter was energetic but not wholly successful. He appeared to have a fixed idea that the Italian language was one easily mastered by the simple method of saying 'da' instead of 'the', and tacking on a final 'a' to any word that seemed to him to need one.

'Say, kid,' he began, 'has da rent-a-man come yet-a?'

The black eyes of the wop kid clouded. He gesticulated, and said something in his native language.

'He hasn't got next,' reported Master Maloney. 'He can't git on to me curves. Dese wop kids is all boneheads. Say, kid, look-a here.' He walked out of the room and closed the door; then, rapping on it smartly from the outside, re-entered and, assuming a look of extreme ferocity, stretched out his hand and thundered: 'Unbelt-a: Slip-a me da stuff!'

The wop kid's puzzlement became pathetic.

'This,' said Psmith, deeply interested, 'is getting about as tense as anything I ever struck. Don't give in, Comrade Maloney. Who knows but that you may yet win through? I fancy the trouble is that your too perfect Italian accent is making the youth home-sick. Once more to the breach, Comrade Maloney.'

Master Maloney made a gesture of disgust. 'I'm t'roo. Dese Dagoes makes me tired. Dey don't know enough to go upstairs to take de Elevated. Beat it, you mutt,' he observed with moody displeasure to the wop kid, accompanying the words with a gesture which conveyed its own meaning. The wop kid, plainly glad to get away, slipped out of the door like a shadow.

Pugsy shrugged his shoulders.

'Gents,' he said resignedly, 'it's up to youse.'

'I fancy,' said Psmith, 'that this is one of those moments when it is necessary for me to unlimber my Sherlock Holmes system. As thus. If the rent collector *had* been here, it is certain, I think, that Comrade Spaghetti, or whatever you said his name was, wouldn't have been. That is to say, if the rent collector had called and found no money waiting for him, surely Comrade Spaghetti would have been out in the cold night instead of under his own roof-tree. Do you follow me, Comrade Maloney?'

'That's right,' said Billy Windsor. 'Of course.'

'Elementary, my dear Watson, elementary,' murmured Psmith.

'So all we have to do is to sit here and wait.'

'All?' said Psmith sadly. 'Surely it is enough. For of all the scaly localities I have struck this seems to me the scaliest. The architect of this Stately Home of America seems to have had a positive hatred of windows. His idea of ventilation was to leave a hole in the wall about the size of a lima bean and let the thing go at that. If our friend does not arrive shortly, I shall pull down the roof. Why, gadzooks! Not to mention stap my vitals! Isn't that a trap-door up there? Make a long-arm, Comrade Windsor.'

Billy got on a chair and pulled the bolt. The trap-door opened downwards. It fell, disclosing a square of deep blue sky.

'Gum!' he said. 'Fancy living in this atmosphere when you don't have to. Fancy these fellows keeping that shut all the time.'

'I expect it is an acquired taste,' said Psmith, 'like Limburger cheese. They don't begin to appreciate air till it is thick enough to scoop chunks out of with a spoon. Then they get up on their hind legs and inflate their chests and say, "This is fine! This beats ozone hollow!" Leave it open, Comrade Windsor. And now, as to the problem of dispensing with Comrade Maloney's services?'

'Sure,' said Billy. 'Beat it, Pugsy, my lad.'

Pugsy looked up, indignant.

'Beat it?' he queried.

'While your shoe leather's good,' said Billy. 'This is no place for a minister's son. There may be a rough house in here any minute, and you would be in the way.'

'I want to stop and pipe de fun,' objected Master Maloney.

'Never mind. Cut off. We'll tell you all about it tomorrow.'

Master Maloney prepared reluctantly to depart. As he did so there was a sound of a well-shod foot on the stairs, and a man in a snuff-coloured suit, wearing a brown Homburg hat and carrying a small notebook in one hand, walked briskly into the room. It was not necessary for Psmith to get his Sherlock Holmes system to work. His whole appearance proclaimed the newcomer to be the long-expected collector of rents.

20. Cornered

He stood in the doorway looking with some surprise at the group inside. He was a smallish, pale-faced man with protruding eyes and teeth which gave him a certain resemblance to a rabbit.

'Hello,' he said.

'Welcome to New York,' said Psmith.

Master Maloney, who had taken advantage of the interruption to edge farther into the room, now appeared to consider the question of his departure permanently shelved. He sidled to a corner and sat down on an empty soap-box with the air of a dramatic critic at the opening night of a new play. The scene looked good to him. It promised interesting developments. Master Maloney was an earnest student of the drama, as exhibited in the theatres of the East Side, and few had ever applauded the hero of 'Escaped from Sing-Sing', or hissed the villain of 'Nellie, the Beautiful Cloak-Model' with more fervour than he. He liked his drama to have plenty of action, and to his practised eye this one promised well. Psmith he looked upon as a quite amiable lunatic, from whom little was to be expected; but there was a set expression on Billy Windsor's face which suggested great things.

His pleasure was abruptly quenched. Billy Windsor, placing a firm hand on his collar, led him to the door and pushed him out, closing the door behind him.

The rent collector watched these things with a puzzled eye. He now turned to Psmith.

'Say, seen anything of the wops that live here?' he inquired.

'I am addressing – ?' said Psmith courteously.

'My name's Gooch.'

Psmith bowed.

'Touching these wops, Comrade Gooch,' he said, 'I fear there is little chance of your seeing them tonight, unless you wait some considerable time. With one of them – the son and heir of the family, I should say – we have just been having a highly interesting and informative chat. Comrade Maloney, who has just left us, acted as interpreter. The father, I am told, is in the dungeon below the castle moat for a brief spell for punching his foreman in the eye. The result? The rent is not forthcoming.'

'Then it's outside for theirs,' said Mr Gooch definitely.

'It's a big shame,' broke in Billy, 'turning the kid out. Where's he to go?'

'That's up to him. Nothing to do with me. I'm only acting under orders from up top.'

'Whose orders, Comrade Gooch?' inquired Psmith.

'The gent who owns this joint.'

'Who is he?' said Billy.

Suspicion crept into the protruding eyes of the rent collector. He waxed wroth.

'Say!' he demanded. 'Who are you two guys, anyway, and what do you think you're doing here? That's what I'd like to know. What do you want with the name of the owner of this place? What business is it of yours?'

'The fact is, Comrade Gooch, we are newspaper men.'

'I guessed you were,' said Mr Gooch with triumph. 'You can't bluff me. Well, it's no good, boys. I've nothing for you. You'd better chase off and try something else.'

He became more friendly.

'Say, though,' he said, 'I just guessed you were from some paper. I wish I could give you a story, but I can't. I guess it's this *Cosy Moments* business that's been and put your editor on to this joint, ain't it? Say, though, that's a queer thing, that paper. Why, only a few weeks ago it used to be a sort of take-home-and-read-to-the-kids affair. A friend of mine used to buy it regular. And then suddenly it comes out with a regular whoop, and started knocking these tenements and boosting Kid Brady, and all that. I can't understand it. All I know is that it's begun to get this place talked about. Why, you see for yourselves how it is. Here is your editor sending you down to get a story about it. But, say, those *Cosy Moments* guys are taking big risks. I tell you straight they are, and that goes. I happen to know a thing or two about what's going on on the other side, and I tell you there's going to be something doing if they don't cut it out quick. Mr – ' he stopped and chuckled, 'Mr – Jones isn't the man to sit still and smile. He's going to get busy. Say, what paper do you boys come from?'

'*Cosy Moments,* Comrade Gooch,' Psmith replied. 'Immediately behind you, between you and the door, is Comrade Windsor, our editor. I am Psmith. I sub-edit.'

For a moment the inwardness of the information did not seem to come home to Mr Gooch. Then it hit him. He spun round. Billy Windsor was standing with his back against the door and a more than nasty look on his face.

'What's all this?' demanded Mr Gooch.

'I will explain all,' said Psmith soothingly. 'In the first place, however, this matter of Comrade Spaghetti's rent. Sooner than see that friend of my boyhood slung out to do the wandering-child-in-the-show act, I will brass up for him.'

'Confound his rent. Let me out.'

'Business before pleasure. How much is it? Twelve dollars? For the privilege of suffocating in this compact little Black Hole? By my halidom, Comrade Gooch, that gentleman whose name you are so shortly to tell us has a very fair idea of how to charge! But who am I that I should criticize? Here are the simoleons, as our young friend, Comrade Maloney, would call them. Push me over a receipt.'

'Let me out.'

'Anon, gossip, anon. – Shakespeare. First, the receipt.'

Mr Gooch scribbled a few words in his notebook and tore out the page. Psmith thanked him.

'I will see that it reaches Comrade Spaghetti,' he said. 'And now to a more important matter. Don't put away that notebook. Turn to a clean page, moisten your pencil, and write as follows. Are you ready? By the way, what is your Christian name? ... Gooch, Gooch, this is no way to speak! Well, if you are sensitive on the point, we will waive the Christian name. It is my duty to tell you, however, that I suspect it to be Percy. Let us push on. Are you ready, once more? Pencil moistened? Very well, then. "I" – comma – "being of sound mind and body" – comma – "and a bright little chap altogether" – comma – Why you're not writing.'

'Let me out,' bellowed Mr Gooch. 'I'll summon you for assault and battery. Playing a fool game like this! Get away from that door.'

'There has been no assault and battery – yet, Comrade Gooch, but who shall predict how long so happy a state of things will last? Do not be deceived by our gay and smiling faces, Comrade Gooch. We mean business. Let me put the whole position of affairs before you; and I am sure a man of your perception will see that there is only one thing to be done.'

He dusted the only chair in the room with infinite care and sat down. Billy Windsor, who had not spoken a word or moved an inch since the beginning of the interview, continued to stand and be silent. Mr Gooch shuffled restlessly in the middle of the room.

'As you justly observed a moment ago,' said Psmith, 'the staff of *Cosy Moments* is taking big risks. We do not rely on your unsupported word for that. We have had practical demonstration of the fact from one J. Repetto, who tried some few nights ago to put us out of business. Well, it struck us both that we had better get hold of the name of the blighter who runs these tenements as quickly as possible, before Comrade Repetto's next night out. That is what we should like you to give us, Comrade Gooch. And we should like it in writing. And, on second thoughts, in ink. I have one of those patent non-leakable fountain pens in my pocket. The Old Journalist's Best Friend. Most of the ink has come out and is permeating the lining of my coat, but I think there is still sufficient for our needs. Remind me later, Comrade Gooch, to continue on the subject of fountain pens. I have much to say on the theme. Meanwhile, however, business, business. That is the cry.'

He produced a pen and an old letter, the last page of which was blank, and began to write.

'How does this strike you?' he said. ' "I" – (I have left a blank for the Christian name: you can write it in yourself later) – "I, blank Gooch, being a collector of rents in Pleasant Street, New York, do hereby swear" – hush, Comrade Gooch, there is no need to do it yet – "that the name of the owner of the Pleasant Street tenements, who is responsible for the perfectly foul conditions there, is – " And that is where you come in, Comrade Gooch. That is where we need your specialized knowledge. Who is he?'

Billy Windsor reached out and grabbed the rent collector by the collar. Having done this, he proceeded to shake him.

Billy was muscular, and his heart was so much in the business that Mr Gooch behaved as if he had been caught in a high wind. It is probable that in another moment the desired information might have been shaken out of him, but before this could happen there was a banging at the door, followed by the entrance of Master Maloney. For the first time since Psmith had known him, Pugsy was openly excited.

'Say,' he began, 'youse had better beat it quick, you had. Dey's coming!'

'And now go back to the beginning, Comrade Maloney,' said Psmith patiently, 'which in the exuberance of the moment you have skipped. Who are coming?'

'Why, dem. De guys.'

Psmith shook his head.

'Your habit of omitting essentials, Comrade Maloney, is going to undo you one of these days. When you get to that ranch of yours, you will probably start out to gallop after the cattle without remembering to mount your mustang. There are four million guys in New York. Which section is it that is coming?'

'Gum! I don't know how many dere is ob dem. I seen Spider Reilly an' Jack Repetto an' – '

'Say no more,' said Psmith. 'If Comrade Repetto is there, that is enough for me. I am going to get on the roof and pull it up after me.'

Billy released Mr Gooch, who fell, puffing, on to the low bed, which stood in one corner of the room.

'They must have spotted us as we were coming here,' he said, 'and followed us. Where did you see them, Pugsy?'

'On de street just outside. Dere was a bunch of dem talkin' togedder, and I hears dem say you was in here. One of dem seen you come in, and dere ain't no ways out but de front, so dey ain't hurryin'! Dey just reckon to pike along upstairs, lookin' into each room till dey finds you. An dere's a bunch of dem goin' to wait on de street in case youse beat it past down de stairs while de udder guys is rubberin' for youse. Say, gents, it's pretty fierce, dis proposition. What are youse goin' to do?'

Mr Gooch, from the bed, laughed unpleasantly.

'I guess you ain't the only assault-and-batter artists in the business,' he said. 'Looks to me as if someone else was going to get shaken up some.'

Billy looked at Psmith.

'Well?' he said, 'What shall we do? Go down and try and rush through?'

Psmith shook his head.

'Not so, Comrade Windsor, but about as much otherwise as you can jolly well imagine.'

'Well, what then?'

'We will stay here. Or rather we will hop nimbly up on to the roof through that skylight. Once there, we may engage these varlets on fairly equal terms. They can only get through one at a time. And while they are doing it I will give my celebrated imitation of Horatius. We had better be moving. Our luggage, fortunately, is small. Merely Comrade Gooch. If you will get through the skylight, I will pass him up to you.'

Mr Gooch, with much verbal embroidery, stated that he would not go. Psmith acted promptly. Gripping the struggling rent collector round the waist, and ignoring his frantic kicks as mere errors in taste, he lifted him to the trap-door, whence the head, shoulders and arms of Billy Windsor protruded into the room. Billy collected the collector, and then Psmith turned to Pugsy.

'Comrade Maloney.'

'Huh?'

'Have I your ear?'

118

'Huh?'

'Are you listening till you feel that your ears are the size of footballs? Then drink this in. For weeks you have been praying for a chance to show your devotion to the great cause; or if you haven't, you ought to have been. That chance has come. You alone can save us. In a sense, of course, we do not need to be saved. They will find it hard to get at us, I fancy, on the roof. But it ill befits the dignity of the editorial staff of a great New York weekly to roost like pigeons for any length of time; and consequently it is up to you.'

'Shall I go for de cops, Mr Smith?'

'No, Comrade Maloney, I thank you. I have seen the cops in action, and they did not impress me. We do not want allies who will merely shake their heads at Comrade Repetto and the others, however sternly. We want someone who will swoop down upon these merry roisterers, and, as it were, soak to them good. Do you know where Dude Dawson lives?'

The light of intelligence began to shine in Master Maloney's face. His eye glistened with respectful approval. This was strategy of the right sort.

'Dude Dawson? Nope. But I can ask around.'

'Do so, Comrade Maloney. And when found, tell him that his old college chum, Spider Reilly, is here. He will not be able to come himself, I fear, but he can send representatives.'

'Sure.'

'That's all, then. Go downstairs with a gay and jaunty air, as if you had no connexion with the old firm at all. Whistle a few lively bars. Make careless gestures. Thus shall you win through. And now it would be no bad idea, I fancy, for me to join the rest of the brains of the paper up aloft. Off you go, Comrade Maloney. And, in passing, don't take a week about it. Leg it with all the speed you possess.'

Pugsy vanished, and Psmith closed the door behind him. Inspection revealed the fact that it possessed no lock. As a barrier it was useless. He left it ajar, and, jumping up, gripped the edge of the opening in the roof and pulled himself through.

Billy Windsor was seated comfortably on Mr Gooch's chest a few feet away. By his side was his big stick. Psmith possessed himself of this, and looked about him. The examination was satisfactory. The trap-door appeared to be the only means of access to the roof, and between their roof and that of the next house there was a broad gulf.

'Practically impregnable,' he murmured. 'Only one thing can dish us, Comrade Windsor; and that is if they have the sense to get on to the roof next door and start shooting. Even in that case, however, we have cover in the shape of the chimneys. I think we may fairly say that all is well. How are you getting along? Has the patient responded at all?'

'Not yet,' said Billy. 'But he's going to.'

'He will be in your charge. I must devote myself exclusively to guarding the bridge. It is a pity that the trap has not got a bolt this side. If it had, the thing would be a perfect picnic. As it is, we must leave it open. But we mustn't expect everything.'

Billy was about to speak, but Psmith suddenly held up his hand warningly. From the room below came a sound of feet.

For a moment the silence was tense. Then from Mr Gooch's lips there escaped a screech.

'This way! They're up –'

The words were cut short as Billy banged his hand over the speaker's mouth. But the thing was done.

'On top de roof,' cried a voice. 'Dey've beaten it for de roof.'

The chair rasped over the floor. Feet shuffled. And then, like a jack-in-the-box, there popped through the opening a head and shoulders.

21. The Battle of Pleasant Street

The new arrival was a young man with a shock of red hair, an ingrowing Roman nose, and a mouth from which force or the passage of time had removed three front teeth. He held on to the edges of the trap with his hands, and stared in a glassy manner into Psmith's face, which was within a foot of his own.

There was a momentary pause, broken by an oath from Mr Gooch, who was still undergoing treatment in the background.

'Aha!' said Psmith genially. 'Historic picture. "Doctor Cook discovers the North Pole." '

The red-headed young man blinked. The strong light of the open air was trying to his eyes.

'Youse had better come down,' he observed coldly. 'We've got youse.'

'And,' continued Psmith, unmoved, 'is instantly handed a gum-drop by his faithful Esquimaux.'

As he spoke, he brought the stick down on the knuckles which disfigured the edges of the trap. The intruder uttered a howl and dropped out of sight. In the room below there were whisperings and mutterings, growing gradually louder till something resembling coherent conversation came to Psmith's ears, as he knelt by the trap making meditative billiard-shots with the stick at a small pebble.

'Aw g'wan! Don't be a quitter!'

'Who's a quitter?'

'Youse a quitter. Get on top de roof. He can't hoit youse.'

'De guy's gotten a big stick.'

Psmith nodded appreciatively.

'I and Roosevelt,' he murmured.

A somewhat baffled silence on the part of the attacking force was followed by further conversation.

'Gum! some guy's got to go up.'

Murmur of assent from the audience.

A voice, in inspired tones: 'Let Sam do it!'

This suggestion made a hit. There was no doubt about that. It was a success from the start. Quite a little chorus of voices expressed sincere approval of the very happy solution, to what had seemed an insoluble problem. Psmith, listening from above, failed to detect in the choir of glad voices one that might belong to Sam himself. Probably gratification had rendered the chosen one dumb.

'Yes, let Sam do it!' cried the unseen chorus. The first speaker, unnecessarily, perhaps – for the motion had been carried almost unanimously – but possibly with the idea of convincing the one member of the party in whose bosom doubts might conceivably be harboured, went on to adduce reasons.

'Sam bein' a coon,' he argued, 'ain't goin' to git hoit by no stick. Youse can't hoit a coon by soakin' him on de coco, can you, Sam?'

Psmith waited with some interest for the reply, but it did not come. Possibly Sam did not wish to generalize on insufficient experience.

'*Solvitur ambulando*,' said Psmith softly, turning the stick round in his fingers. 'Comrade Windsor!'

'Hullo!'

'Is it possible to hurt a coloured gentleman by hitting him on the head with a stick?'

'If you hit him hard enough.'

'I knew there was some way out of the difficulty,' said Psmith with satisfaction. 'How are you getting on up at your end of the table, Comrade Windsor?'

'Fine.'

'Any result yet?'

'Not at present.'

'Don't give up.'

'Not me.'

'The right spirit, Comrade Win –'

A report like a cannon in the room below interrupted him. It was merely a revolver shot, but in the confined space it was deafening. The bullet sang up into the sky.

'Never hit me!' said Psmith with dignified triumph.

The noise was succeeded by a shuffling of feet. Psmith grasped his stick more firmly. This was evidently the real attack. The revolver shot had been a mere demonstration of artillery to cover the infantry's advance.

Sure enough, the next moment a woolly head popped through the opening, and a pair of rolling eyes gleamed up at the old Etonian.

'Why, Sam!' said Psmith cordially, 'this is well met! I remember *you*. Yes, indeed, I do. Wasn't you the feller with the open umbereller that I met one rainy morning on the Av-en-ue? What, are you coming up? Sam, I hate to do it, but – '

A yell rang out.

'What was that?' asked Billy Windsor over his shoulder.

'Your statement, Comrade Windsor, has been tested and proved correct.'

By this time the affair had begun to draw a 'gate'. The noise of the revolver had proved a fine advertisement. The roof of the house next door began to fill up. Only a few occupants could get a clear view of the proceedings, for a large chimney-stack intervened. There was considerable speculation as to what was passing between Billy Windsor and Mr Gooch. Psmith's share in the entertainment was more obvious. The early comers had seen his interview with Sam, and were relating it with gusto to their friends. Their attitude towards Psmith was that of a group of men watching a terrier at a rat-hole. They looked to him to provide entertainment for them, but they realized that the first move must be with the attackers. They were fair-minded men, and they did not expect Psmith to make any aggressive move.

Their indignation, when the proceedings began to grow slow, was directed entirely at the dilatory Three Pointers. With an aggrieved air, akin to that of a crowd at a cricket match when batsmen are playing for a draw, they began to 'barrack'. They hooted the Three Pointers. They begged them to go home and tuck themselves up in bed. The men on the roof were mostly Irishmen, and it offended them to see what should have been a spirited fight so grossly bungled.

'G'wan away home, ye quitters!' roared one.

'Call yersilves the Three Points, do ye? An' would ye know what *I* call ye? The Young Ladies' Seminary!' bellowed another with withering scorn.

A third member of the audience alluded to them as 'stiffs'.

'I fear, Comrade Windsor,' said Psmith, 'that our blithe friends below are beginning to grow a little unpopular with the many-headed. They must be up and doing if they wish to retain the esteem of Pleasant Street. Aha!'

Another and a longer explosion from below, and more bullets wasted themselves on air. Psmith sighed.

'They make me tired,' he said. 'This is no time for a *feu de joie*. Action! That is the cry. Action! Get busy, you blighters!'

The Irish neighbours expressed the same sentiment in different and more forcible words. There was no doubt about it – as warriors, the Three Pointers had failed to give satisfaction.

A voice from the room called up to Psmith.

'Say!'

'You have our ear,' said Psmith.

'What's that?'

'I said you had our ear.'

'Are youse stiffs comin' down off out of dat roof?'

'Would you mind repeating that remark?'

'Are youse guys goin' to quit off out of dat roof?'

'Your grammar is perfectly beastly,' said Psmith severely.

'Hey!'

'Well?'

'Are youse guys – ?'

'No, my lad,' said Psmith, 'since you ask, we are not. And why? Because the air up here is refreshing, the view pleasant, and we are expecting at any moment an important communication from Comrade Gooch.'

'We're goin' to wait here till youse come down.'

'If you wish it,' said Psmith courteously, 'by all means do.

Who am I that I should dictate your movements? The most I aspire to is to check them when they take an upward direction.'

There was silence below. The time began to pass slowly. The Irishmen on the other roof, now definitely abandoning hope of further entertainment, proceeded with hoots of scorn to climb down one by one into the recesses of their own house.

Suddenly from the street far below there came a fusillade of shots and a babel of shouts and counter-shouts. The roof of the house next door, which had been emptying itself slowly and reluctantly, filled again with a magical swiftness, and the low wall facing into the street became black with the backs of those craning over.

'What's that?' inquired Billy.

'I rather fancy,' said Psmith, 'that our allies of the Table Hill contingent must have arrived. I sent Comrade Maloney to explain matters to Dude Dawson, and it seems as if that golden-hearted sportsman has responded. There appear to be great doings in the street.'

In the room below confusion had arisen. A scout, clattering upstairs, had brought the news of the Table Hillites' advent, and there was doubt as to the proper course to pursue. Certain voices urged going down to help the main body. Others pointed out that that would mean abandoning the siege of the roof. The scout who had brought the news was eloquent in favour of the first course.

'Gum!' he cried, 'don't I keep tellin' youse dat de Table Hills is here? Sure, dere's a whole bunch of dem, and unless youse come on down dey'll bite de hull head off of us lot. Leave those stiffs on de roof. Let Sam wait here with his canister, and den dey can't get down, 'cos Sam'll pump dem full of lead while dey're beatin' it t'roo de trap-door. Sure.'

Psmith nodded reflectively.

'There is certainly something in what the bright boy says,' he murmured. 'It seems to me the grand rescue scene in the third act has sprung a leak. This will want thinking over.'

In the street the disturbance had now become terrific. Both sides were hard at it, and the Irishmen on the roof, rewarded at last for their long vigil, were yelling encouragement promiscuously and whooping with the unfettered ecstasy of men who are getting the treat of their lives without having paid a penny for it.

The behaviour of the New York policeman in affairs of this kind is based on principles of the soundest practical wisdom. The unthinking man would rush in and attempt to crush the combat in its earliest and fiercest stages. The New York policeman, knowing the importance of his own safety, and the insignificance of the gangsman's, permits the opposing forces to hammer each other into a certain distaste for battle, and then, when both sides have begun to have enough of it, rushes in himself and clubs everything in sight. It is an admirable process in its results, but it is sure rather than swift.

Proceedings in the affair below had not yet reached the police interference stage. The noise, what with the shots and yells from the street and the ear-piercing approval of the roof-audience, was just working up to a climax.

Psmith rose. He was tired of kneeling by the trap, and there was no likelihood of Sam making another attempt to climb through. He walked towards Billy.

As he did so, Billy got up and turned to him. His eyes were gleaming with excitement. His whole attitude was triumphant. In his hand he waved a strip of paper.

'I've got it,' he cried.

'Excellent, Comrade Windsor,' said Psmith. 'Surely we must win through now. All we have to do is to get off this roof, and fate cannot touch us. Are two mammoth minds such as ours unequal to such a feat? It can hardly be. Let us ponder.'

'Why not go down through the trap? They've all gone to the street.'

Psmith shook his head.

'All,' he replied, 'save Sam. Sam was the subject of my late successful experiment, when I proved that coloured gentlemen's heads could be hurt with a stick. He is now waiting below, armed with a pistol, ready – even anxious – to pick us off as we climb through the trap. How would it be to drop Comrade Gooch through first, and so draw his fire? Comrade Gooch, I am sure, would be delighted to do a little thing like that for old friends of our standing or – but what's that!'

'What's the matter?'

Is that a ladder that I see before me, its handle to my hand? It is! Comrade Windsor, we win through. *Cosy Moments'* editorial staff may be tree'd, but it cannot be put out of business. Comrade Windsor, take the other end of that ladder and follow me.'

The ladder was lying against the farther wall. It was long, more than enough for the purpose for which it was needed. Psmith and Billy rested it on the coping, and pushed it till the other end reached across the gulf to the roof of the house next door, Mr Gooch eyeing them in silence the while.

Psmith turned to him.

'Comrade Gooch,' he said, 'do nothing to apprise our friend Sam of these proceedings. I speak in your best interests. Sam is in no mood to make nice distinctions between friend and foe. If you bring him up here, he will probably mistake you for a member of the staff of *Cosy Moments,* and loose off in your direction without waiting for explanations. I think you had better come with us. I will go first, Comrade Windsor, so that if the ladder breaks, the paper will lose merely a sub-editor, not an editor.'

He went down on all-fours, and in this attitude wormed his way across to the opposite roof, whose occupants, engrossed in the fight in the street, in which the police had now joined, had their backs turned and did not observe him. Mr Gooch, pallid and obviously ill-attuned to such feats, followed him; and finally Billy Windsor reached the other side.

'Neat,' said Psmith complacently. 'Uncommonly neat. Comrade Gooch reminded me of the untamed chamois of the Alps, leaping from crag to crag.'

In the street there was now comparative silence. The police, with their clubs, had knocked the last remnant of fight out of the combatants. Shooting had definitely ceased.

'I think,' said Psmith, 'that we might now descend. If you have no other engagements, Comrade Windsor, I will take you to the Knickerbocker, and buy you a square meal. I would ask for the pleasure of your company also, Comrade Gooch, were it not that matters of private moment, relating to the policy of the paper, must be discussed at the table. Some other day, perhaps. We are infinitely obliged to you for your sympathetic cooperation in this little matter. And now good-bye. Comrade Windsor, let us debouch.'

22. Concerning Mr Waring

Psmith pushed back his chair slightly, stretched out his legs, and lit a cigarette. The resources of the Knickerbocker Hotel had proved equal to supplying the fatigued staff of *Cosy Moments* with an excellent dinner, and Psmith had stoutly declined to talk business until the coffee arrived. This had been hard on Billy, who was bursting with his news. Beyond a hint that it was sensational he had not been permitted to go.

'More bright young careers than I care to think of,' said Psmith, 'have been ruined by the fatal practice of talking shop at dinner. But now that we are through, Comrade Windsor, by all means let us have it. What's the name which Comrade Gooch so eagerly divulged?'

Billy leaned forward excitedly.

'Stewart Waring,' he whispered.

'Stewart who?' asked Psmith.

Billy stared.

'Great Scott, man!' he said, 'haven't you heard of Stewart Waring?'

'The name seems vaguely familiar, like isinglass or Post-toasties. I seem to know it, but it conveys nothing to me.'

'Don't you ever read the papers?'

'I toy with my *American* of a morning, but my interest is confined mainly to the sporting page which reminds me that Comrade Brady has been matched against one Eddie Wood a month from today. Gratifying as it is to find one of the staff getting on in life, I fear this will cause us a certain amount of inconvenience. Comrade Brady will have to leave the office temporarily in order to go into training, and what shall we do then for a fighting editor? However, possibly we may not need one now. *Cosy Moments* should be able shortly to give its message to the world and ease up for a while. Which brings us back to the point. Who is Stewart Waring?'

'Stewart Waring is running for City Alderman. He's one of the biggest men in New York!'

'Do you mean in girth? If so, he seems to have selected the right career for himself.'

'He's one of the bosses. He used to be Commissioner of Buildings for the city.'

'Commissioner of Buildings? What exactly did that let him in for?'

'It let him in for a lot of graft.'

'How was that?'

'Oh, he took it off the contractors. Shut his eyes and held out his hands when they ran up rotten buildings that a strong breeze would have knocked down, and places like that Pleasant Street hole without any ventilation.'

'Why did he throw up the job?' inquired Psmith. 'It seems to me that it was among the World's Softest. Certain drawbacks to it, perhaps, to the man with the Hair-Trigger Conscience; but I gather that Comrade Waring did not line up in that class. What was his trouble?'

'His trouble,' said Billy, 'was that he stood in with a contractor who was putting up a music-hall, and the contractor put it up with material about as strong as a heap of meringues, and it collapsed on the third night and killed half the audience.'

'And then?'

'The papers raised a howl, and they got after the contractor, and the contractor gave Waring away. It killed him for the time being.'

'I should have thought it would have had that excellent result permanently,' said Psmith thoughtfully. 'Do you mean to say he got back again after that?'

'He had to quit being Commissioner, of course, and leave the town for a time; but affairs move so fast here that a thing like that blows over. He made a bit of a pile out of the job, and could afford to lie low for a year or two.'

'How long ago was that?'

'Five years. People don't remember a thing here that happened five years back unless they're reminded of it.'

Psmith lit another cigarette.

'We will remind them,' he said.

Billy nodded.

'Of course,' he said, 'one or two of the papers against him in this Aldermanic Election business tried to bring the thing up, but they didn't cut any ice. The other papers said it was a shame, hounding a man who was sorry for the past and who was trying to make good now; so they dropped it. Everybody thought that Waring was on the level now. He's been shooting off a lot of hot air lately about philanthropy and so on. Not that he has actually done a thing – not so much as given a supper to a dozen news-boys; but he's talked, and talk gets over if you keep it up long enough.'

Psmith nodded adhesion to this dictum.

'So that naturally he wants to keep it dark about these tenements. It'll smash him at the election when it gets known.'

'Why is he so set on becoming an Alderman?' inquired Psmith.

'There's a lot of graft to being an Alderman,' explained Billy.

'I see. No wonder the poor gentleman was so energetic in his methods. What is our move now, Comrade Windsor?'

Billy stared.

'Why, publish the name, of course.'

'But before then? How are we going to ensure the safety of our evidence? We stand or fall entirely by that slip of paper, because we've got the beggar's name in the writing of his own collector, and that's proof positive.'

'That's all right,' said Billy, patting his breast-pocket. 'Nobody's going to get it from me.'

Psmith dipped his hand into his trouser-pocket.

'Comrade Windsor,' he said, producing a piece of paper, 'how do we go?'

He leaned back in his chair, surveying Billy blandly through his eye-glass. Billy's eyes were goggling. He looked from Psmith to the paper and from the paper to Psmith.

'What – what the – ?' he stammered. 'Why, it's *it*!'

Psmith nodded.

'How on earth did you get it?'

Psmith knocked the ash off his cigarette.

'Comrade Windsor,' he said, 'I do not wish to cavil or carp or rub it in in any way. I will merely remark that you pretty nearly landed us in the soup, and pass on to more congenial topics. Didn't you know we were followed to this place?'

'Followed!'

'By a merchant in what Comrade Maloney would call a tall-shaped hat. I spotted him at an early date, somewhere down by Twenty-ninth Street. When we dived into Sixth Avenue for a space at Thirty-third Street, did he dive, too? He did. And when we turned into Forty-second Street, there he was. I tell you, Comrade Windsor, leeches were aloof, and burrs non-adhesive compared with that tall-shaped-hatted blighter.'

'Yes?'

'Do you remember, as you came to the entrance of this place, somebody knocking against you?'

'Yes, there was a pretty big crush in the entrance.'

'There was; but not so big as all that. There was plenty of room for this merchant to pass if he had wished. Instead of which he butted into you. I happened to be waiting for just that, so I managed to attach myself to his wrist with some vim and give it a fairly hefty wrench. The paper was inside his hand.'

Billy was leaning forward with a pale face.

'Jove!' he muttered.

'That about sums it up,' said Psmith.

Billy snatched the paper from the table and extended it towards him.

'Here,' he said feverishly, 'you take it. Gum, I never thought I was such a mutt! I'm not fit to take charge of a toothpick. Fancy me not being on the watch for something of that sort. I guess I was so tickled with myself at the thought of having got the thing, that it never struck me they might try for it. But I'm through. No more for me. You're the man in charge now.'

Psmith shook his head.

'These stately compliments,' he said, 'do my old heart good, but I fancy I know a better plan. It happened that I chanced to have my eye on the blighter in the tall-shaped hat, and so was enabled to land him among the ribstons; but who knows but that in the crowd on Broadway there may not lurk others, unidentified blighters in equally tall-shaped hats, one of whom may work the same sleight-of-hand speciality on me? It was not that you were not capable of taking care of that paper: it was simply that you didn't happen to spot the man. Now observe me closely, for what follows is an exhibition of Brain.'

He paid the bill, and they went out into the entrance-hall of the hotel. Psmith, sitting down at a table, placed the paper in an envelope and addressed it to himself at the address of *Cosy Moments*. After which, he stamped the envelope and dropped it into the letter-box at the back of the hall.

'And now, Comrade Windsor,' he said, 'let us stroll gently homewards down the Great White Way. What matter though it be fairly stiff with low-browed bravoes in tall-shaped hats? They cannot harm us. From me, if they search me thoroughly, they may scoop a matter of eleven dollars, a watch, two stamps, and a packet of chewing-gum. Whether they would do any better with you I do not know. At any rate, they wouldn't get that paper; and that's the main thing.'

'You're a genius,' said Billy Windsor.

'You think so?' said Psmith diffidently. 'Well, well, perhaps you are right, perhaps you are right. Did you notice the hired ruffian in the flannel suit who just passed? He wore a slightly baffled look, I fancy. And hark! Wasn't that a muttered "Failed!" I heard? Or was it the breeze moaning in the tree-tops? Tonight is a cold, disappointing night for Hired Ruffians, Comrade Windsor.'

23. Reductions in the Staff

The first member of the staff of *Cosy Moments* to arrive at the office on the following morning was Master Maloney. This sounds like the beginning of a 'Plod and Punctuality', or 'How Great Fortunes have been Made' story; but, as a matter of fact, Master Maloney was no early bird. Larks who rose in his neighbourhood, rose alone. He did not get up with them. He was supposed to be at the office at nine o'clock. It was a point of honour with him, a sort of daily declaration of independence, never to put in an appearance before nine-thirty. On this particular morning he was punctual to the minute, or half an hour late, whichever way you choose to look at it.

He had only whistled a few bars of 'My Little Irish Rose', and had barely got into the first page of his story of life on the prairie when Kid Brady appeared. The Kid, as was his habit when not in training, was smoking a big black cigar. Master Maloney eyed him admiringly. The Kid, unknown to that gentleman himself, was Pugsy's ideal. He came from the Plains, and had, indeed, once actually been a cowboy; he was a coming champion; and he could smoke black cigars. It was, therefore, without his usual well-what-is-it-now? air that Pugsy laid down his book, and prepared to converse.

'Say, Mr Smith or Mr Windsor about, Pugsy?' asked the Kid.

'Naw, Mr Brady, they ain't came yet,' replied Master Maloney respectfully.

'Late, ain't they?'

'Sure. Mr Windsor generally blows in before I do.'

'Wonder what's keepin' them.'

'P'raps, dey've bin put out of business,' suggested Pugsy nonchalantly.

How's that?'

Pugsy related the events of the previous day, relaxing something of his austere calm as he did so. When he came to the part where the Table Hill allies swooped down on the unsuspecting Three Pointers, he was almost animated.

'Say,' said the Kid approvingly, 'that Smith guy's got more grey matter under his hatch than you'd think to look at him. I –'

'Comrade Brady,' said a voice in the doorway, 'you do me proud.'

'Why, say,' said the Kid, turning, 'I guess the laugh's on me. I didn't see you, Mr Smith. Pugsy's bin tellin' me how you sent him for the Table Hills yesterday. That was cute. It was mighty smart. But say, those guys are goin' some, ain't they now! Seems as if they was dead set on puttin' you out of business.'

'Their manner yesterday, Comrade Brady, certainly suggested the presence of some sketchy outline of such an ideal in their minds. One Sam, in particular, an ebony-hued sportsman, threw himself into the task with great vim. I rather fancy he is waiting for us with his revolver at this moment. But why worry? Here we are, safe and sound, and Comrade Windsor may be expected to arrive at any moment. I see, Comrade Brady, that you have been matched against one Eddie Wood.'

'It's about that I wanted to see you, Mr Smith. Say, now that things have been and brushed up so, what with these gang guys layin' for you the way they're doin', I guess you'll be needin' me around here. Isn't that right? Say the word and I'll call off this Eddie Wood fight.'

'Comrade Brady,' said Psmith with some enthusiasm, 'I call that a sporting offer. I'm very much obliged. But we mustn't stand in your way. If you eliminate this Comrade Wood, they will have to give you a chance against Jimmy Garvin, won't they?'

'I guess that's right, sir,' said the Kid. 'Eddie stayed nineteen rounds against Jimmy, and if I can put him away, it gets me into line with Jimmy, and he can't side-step me.'

'Then go in and win, Comrade Brady. We shall miss you. It will be as if a ray of sunshine had been removed from the office But you mustn't throw a chance away. We shall be all right, I think.'

'I'll train at White Plains,' said the Kid. 'That ain't far from here, so I'll be pretty near in case I'm wanted. Hullo, who's here?'

He pointed to the door. A small boy was standing there, holding a note.

'Mr Smith?'

'Sir to you,' said Psmith courteously.

'P. Smith?'

'The same. This is your lucky day.'

'Cop at Jefferson Market give me dis to take to youse.'

'A cop in Jefferson Market?' repeated Psmith. 'I did not know I had friends among the constabulary there. Why, it's from Comrade Windsor.' He opened the envelope and read the letter. 'Thanks,' he said, giving the boy a quarter-dollar.

It was apparent the Kid was politely endeavouring to veil his curiosity. Master Maloney had no such scruples.

'What's in de letter, boss?' he inquired.

'The letter, Comrade Maloney, is from our Mr Windsor, and relates in terse language the following facts, that our editor last night hit a policeman in the eye, and that he was sentenced this morning to thirty days on Blackwell's Island.'

'He's de guy!' admitted Master Maloney approvingly.

'What's that?' said the Kid. 'Mr Windsor bin punchin' cops! What's he bin doin' that for?'

'He gives no clue. I must go and find out. Could you help Comrade Maloney mind the shop for a few moments while I push round to Jefferson Market and make inquiries?'

'Sure. But say, fancy Mr Windsor cuttin' loose that way!' said the Kid admiringly.

The Jefferson Market Police Court is a little way down town, near Washington Square. It did not take Psmith long to reach it, and by the judicious expenditure of a few dollars he was enabled to obtain an interview with Billy in a back room.

The chief editor of *Cosy Moments* was seated on a bench

looking upon the world through a pair of much blackened eyes. His general appearance was dishevelled. He had the air of a man who has been caught in the machinery.

'Hullo, Smith,' he said. 'You got my note all right then?'

Psmith looked at him, concerned.

'Comrade Windsor,' he said, 'what on earth has been happening to you?'

'Oh, that's all right,' said Billy. 'That's nothing.'

'Nothing! You look as if you had been run over by a motor-car.'

'The cops did that,' said Billy, without any apparent resentment. 'They always turn nasty if you put up a fight. I was a fool to do it, I suppose, but I got so mad. They knew perfectly well that I had nothing to do with any pool-room downstairs.'

Psmith's eye-glass dropped from his eye.

'Pool-room, Comrade Windsor?'

'Yes. The house where I live was raided late last night. It seems that some gamblers have been running a pool-room on the ground floor. Why the cops should have thought I had anything to do with it, when I was sleeping peacefully upstairs, is more than I can understand. Anyway, at about three in the morning there was the dickens of a banging at my door. I got up to see what was doing, and found a couple of policemen there. They told me to come along with them to the station. I asked what on earth for. I might have known it was no use arguing with a New York cop. They said they had been tipped off that there was a pool-room being run in the house, and that they were cleaning up the house, and if I wanted to say anything I'd better say it to the magistrate. I said, all right, I'd put on some clothes and come with them. They said they couldn't wait about while I put on clothes. I said I wasn't going to travel about New York in pyjamas, and started to get into my shirt. One of them gave me a shove in the ribs with his night-stick, and told me to come along quick. And that made me so mad I hit out.' A chuckle escaped Billy. 'He wasn't expecting it, and I got him fair. He went down over the bookcase. The other cop took a swipe at me with his club, but by that time I was so mad I'd have taken on Jim Jeffries, if he had shown up and got in my way. I just sailed in, and was beginning to make the man think that he had stumbled on Stanley Ketchel or Kid Brady or a dynamite explosion by mistake, when the other fellow loosed himself from the bookcase, and they started in on me together, and there was a general rough house, in the middle of which somebody seemed to let off about fifty thousand dollars' worth of fireworks all in a bunch; and I didn't remember anything more till I found myself in a cell, pretty nearly knocked to pieces. That's my little life-history. I guess I was a fool to cut loose that way, but I was so mad I didn't stop to think.'

Psmith sighed.

'You have told me your painful story,' he said. 'Now hear mine. After parting with you last night, I went meditatively back to my Fourth Avenue address, and, with a courtly good night to the large policeman who, as I have mentioned in previous conversations, is stationed almost at my very door, I passed on into my room, and had soon sunk into a dreamless slumber. At about three o'clock in the morning I was aroused by a somewhat hefty banging on the door.'

'What!'

'A banging at the door,' repeated Psmith.

'There, standing on the mat, were three policemen. From their remarks I gathered that certain bright spirits had been running a gambling establishment in the lower regions of the building – where, I think I told you, there is a saloon – and the Law was now about to clean up the place. Very cordially the honest fellows invited me to go with them. A conveyance, it seemed, waited in the street without. I pointed out, even as you appear to have done, that sea-green pyjamas with old rose frogs were not the costume in which a Shropshire Psmith should be seen abroad in one of the world's greatest cities; but they assured me – more by their manner than their words – that my misgivings were out place, so I yielded. These men, I told myself, have lived longer in New York than I. They know what is done and what is not done. I will bow to their views. So I went with them, and after a very pleasant and cosy little ride in the patrol waggon, arrived at the police station. This morning I chatted a while with the courteous magistrate, convinced him by means of arguments and by silent evidence of my open, honest face and unwavering eye that I was not a professional gambler, and came away without a stain on my character.'

Billy Windsor listened to this narrative with growing interest.

'Gum! it's them!' he cried.

'As Comrade Maloney would say,' said Psmith, 'meaning what, Comrade Windsor?'

'Why, the fellows who are after that paper. They tipped the police off about the pool-rooms, knowing that we should be hauled off without having time to take anything with us. I'll bet anything you like they have been in and searched our rooms by now.'

'As regards yours, Comrade Windsor, I cannot say. But it is an undoubted fact that mine, which I revisited before going to the office, in order to correct what seemed to me even on reflection certain drawbacks to my costume, looks as if two cyclones and a threshing machine had passed through it.'

'They've searched it?'

'With a fine-toothed comb. Not one of my objects of vertu but has been displaced.'

Billy Windsor slapped his knee.

'It was lucky you thought of sending that paper by post,' he said. 'We should have been done if you hadn't. But, say,' he went on miserably, 'this is awful. Things are just warming up for the final burst, and I'm out of it all.'

'For thirty days,' sighed Psmith. 'What *Cosy Moments* really needs is a *sitz-redacteur.*'

'A what?'

'A *sitz-redacteur,* Comrade Windsor, is a gentleman employed by German newspapers with a taste for *lèse majesté* to go to prison whenever required in place of the real editor. The real editor hints in his bright and snappy editorial, for instance, that the Kaiser's moustache reminds him of a bad dream. The police force swoops down *en masse* on the office of the journal, and are met by the *sitz-redacteur,* who goes with them peaceably, allowing the editor to remain and sketch out plans for his next week's article on the Crown Prince. We need a *sitz-*

139

redacteur on *Cosy Moments* almost as much as a fighting editor; and we have neither.'

'The Kid has had to leave then?'

'He wants to go into training at once. He very sportingly offered to cancel his match, but of course that would never do. Unless you consider Comrade Maloney equal to the job, I must look around me for some one else. I shall be too fully occupied with purely literary matters to be able to deal with chance callers. But I have a scheme.'

'What's that?'

'It seems to me that we are allowing much excellent material to lie unused in the shape of Comrade Jarvis.'

'Bat Jarvis.'

'The same. The cat-specialist to whom you endeared yourself somewhat earlier in the proceedings by befriending one of his wandering animals. Little deeds of kindness, little acts of love, as you have doubtless heard, help, etc. Should we not give Comrade Jarvis an opportunity of proving the correctness of this statement? I think so. Shortly after you – if you will forgive me for touching on a painful subject – have been haled to your dungeon, I will push round to Comrade Jarvis's address, and sound him on the subject. Unfortunately, his affection is confined, I fancy, to you. Whether he will consent to put himself out on my behalf remains to be seen. However, there is no harm in trying. If nothing else comes of the visit, I shall at least have had the opportunity of chatting with one of our most prominent citizens.'

A policeman appeared at the door.

'Say, pal,' he remarked to Psmith, 'you'll have to be fading away soon, I guess. Give you three minutes more. Say it quick.'

He retired. Billy leaned forward to Psmith.

'I guess they won't give me much chance,' he whispered, 'but if you see me around in the next day or two, don't be surprised.'

'I fail to follow you, Comrade Windsor.'

'Men have escaped from Blackwell's Island before now. Not many, it's true; but it has been done.'

Psmith shook his head.

'I shouldn't,' he said. 'They're bound to catch you, and then you will be immersed in the soup beyond hope of recovery I shouldn't wonder if they put you in your little cell for a year o so.'

'I don't care,' said Billy stoutly. 'I'd give a year later on to be round and about now.'

'I shouldn't,' urged Psmith. 'All will be well with the paper. You have left a good man at the helm.'

'I guess I shan't get a chance; but I'll try it if I do.'

The door opened and the policeman reappeared.

'Time's up, I reckon.'

'Well, good-bye, Comrade Windsor,' said Psmith regretfully. 'Abstain from undue worrying. It's a walk-over from now on, and there's no earthly need for you to be around the office. Once, I admit, this could not have been said. But now things have simplified themselves. Have no fear. This act is going to be a scream from start to finish.'

24. A Gathering of Cat-Specialists

Master Maloney raised his eyes for a moment from his book as Psmith re-entered the office.

'Dere's a guy in dere waitin' ter see youse,' he said briefly, jerking his head in the direction of the inner room.

'A guy waiting to see me, Comrade Maloney? With or without a sand-bag?'

'Says his name's Jackson,' said Master Maloney, turning a page.

Psmith moved quickly to the door of the inner room.

'Why, Comrade Jackson,' he said, with the air of a father welcoming home the prodigal son, 'this is the maddest, merriest day of all the glad New Year. Where did you come from?'

Mike, looking very brown and in excellent condition, put down the paper he was reading.

'Hullo Smith,' he said. 'I got back this morning. We're playing a game over in Brooklyn tomorrow.'

'No engagements of any importance today?'

'Not a thing. Why?'

'Because I propose to take you to visit Comrade Jarvis, whom you will doubtless remember.'

'Jarvis?' said Mike, puzzled. 'I don't remember any Jarvis.'

'Let your mind wander back a little through the jungle of the past. Do you recollect paying a visit to Comrade Windsor's room – '

'By the way, where *is* Windsor?'

'In prison. Well, on that evening – '

'In prison?'

'For thirty days. For slugging a policeman. More of this, however, anon. Let us return to that evening. Don't you remember a certain gentleman with just about enough forehead to keep his front hair from getting all tangled up with his eye-brows – '

'Oh, the cat chap? *I* know.'

'As you very justly observe, Comrade Jackson, the cat chap. For going straight to the mark and seizing on the salient point of a situation I know of no one who can last two minutes against you. Comrade Jarvis may have other sides to his character – possibly many – but it is as a cat chap that I wish to approach him today.'

'What's the idea? What are you going to see him for?'

'We,' corrected Psmith. 'I will explain all at a little luncheon at which I trust that you will be my guest. Already, such is the stress of this journalistic life, I hear my tissues crying out imperatively to be restored. An oyster and a glass of milk somewhere round the corner, Comrade Jackson? I think so, I think so.'

'I was reading *Cosy Moments* in there,' said Mike, as they lunched. 'You certainly seem to have bucked it up rather. Kid Brady's reminiscences are hot stuff.'

'Somewhat sizzling, Comrade Jackson,' admitted Psmith. 'They have, however, unfortunately cost us a fighting editor.'

'How's that?'

'Such is the boost we have given Comrade Brady, that he is now never without a match. He has had to leave us today to go to White Plains to train for an encounter with a certain Mr Wood, a four-ounce-glove juggler of established fame.'

'I expect you need a fighting editor, don't you?'

'He is indispensable, Comrade Jackson, quite indispensable.'

'No rotting. Has anybody cut up rough about the stuff you've printed?'

'Cut up rough? Gadzooks! I need merely say that one critical reader put a bullet through my hat – '

'Rot! Not really?'

'While others kept me tree'd on top of a roof for the space of nearly an hour. Assuredly they have cut up rough, Comrade Jackson.'

'Great Scott! Tell us.'

Psmith briefly recounted the adventures of the past few weeks.

'But, man,' said Mike, when he had finished, 'why on earth don't you call in the police?'

'We have mentioned the matter to certain of the force. They appeared tolerably interested, but showed no tendency to leap excitedly to our assistance. The New York policeman, Comrade Jackson, like all great men, is somewhat peculiar. If you go to a New York policeman and exhibit a black eye, he will examine it and express some admiration for the abilities of the citizen responsible for the same. If you press the matter, he becomes bored, and says, "Ain't youse satisfied with what youse got? G'wan!" His advice in such cases is good, and should be followed. No; since coming to this city I have developed a habit of taking care of myself, or employing private help. That is why I should like you, if you will, to come with me to call upon Comrade Jarvis. He is a person of considerable influence among that section of the populace which is endeavouring to smash in our occiputs. Indeed, I know of nobody who cuts a greater quantity of ice. If I can only enlist Comrade Jarvis's assistance, all will be well. If you are through with your refreshment, shall we be moving in his direction? By the way, it will probably be necessary in the course of our interview to allude to you as one of our most eminent living cat-fanciers. You do not object? Remember that you have in your English home seventy-four fine cats, mostly Angoras. Are you on to that? Then let us be going. Comrade Maloney has given me the address. It is a goodish step down on the East Side. I should like to take a taxi, but it might seem ostentatious. Let us walk.'

They found Mr Jarvis in his Groome Street fancier's shop, engaged in the intellectual occupation of greasing a cat's paws with butter. He looked up as they entered, and began to breathe a melody with a certain coyness.

'Comrade Jarvis,' said Psmith, 'we meet again. You remember me?'

'Nope,' said Mr Jarvis, pausing for a moment in the middle

of a bar, and then taking up the air where he had left off. Psmith was not discouraged.

'Ah,' he said tolerantly, 'the fierce rush of New York life. How it wipes from the retina today the image impressed on it but yesterday. Are you with me, Comrade Jarvis?'

The cat-expert concentrated himself on the cat's paws without replying.

'A fine animal,' said Psmith, adjusting his eyeglass. 'To which particular family of the Felis Domestica does that belong? In colour it resembles a Neapolitan ice more than anything.'

Mr Jarvis's manner became unfriendly.

'Say, what do youse want? That's straight ain't it? If youse want to buy a boid or a snake, why don't youse say so?'

'I stand corrected,' said Psmith. 'I should have remembered that time is money. I called in here partly on the strength of being a colleague and side-partner of Comrade Windsor – '

'Mr Windsor! De gent what caught me cat?'

'The same – and partly in order that I might make two very eminent cat-fanciers acquainted. This,' he said, with a wave of his hand in the direction of the silently protesting Mike, 'is Comrade Jackson, possibly the best known of our English cat-fanciers. Comrade Jackson's stud of Angoras is celebrated wherever the King's English is spoken, and in Hoxton.'

Mr Jarvis rose, and, having inspected Mike with silent admiration for a while, extended a well-buttered hand towards him. Psmith looked on benevolently.

'What Comrade Jackson does not know about cats,' he said, 'is not knowledge. His information on Angoras alone would fill a volume.'

'Say,' – Mr Jarvis was evidently touching on a point which had weighed deeply upon him – 'why's catnip called catnip?'

Mike looked at Psmith helplessly. It sounded like a riddle, but it was obvious that Mr Jarvis's motive in putting the question was not frivolous. He really wished to know.

'The word, as Comrade Jackson was just about to observe,' said Psmith, 'is a corruption of cat-mint. Why it should be so corrupted I do not know. But what of that? The subject is too

145

deep to be gone fully into at the moment. I should recommend you to read Comrade Jackson's little brochure on the matter. Passing lightly on from that – '

'Did youse ever have a cat dat ate beetles?' inquired Mr Jarvis.

'There was a time when many of Comrade Jackson's felidae supported life almost entirely on beetles.'

'Did they git thin?'

Mike felt that it was time, if he was to preserve his reputation, to assert himself.

'No,' he replied firmly.

Mr Jarvis looked astonished.

'English beetles,' said Psmith, 'don't make cats thin. Passing lightly – '

'I had a cat oncest,' said Mr Jarvis, ignoring the remark and sticking to his point, 'dat ate beetles and got thin and used to tie itself inter knots.'

'A versatile animal,' agreed Psmith.

'Say,' Mr Jarvis went on, now plainly on a subject near to his heart, 'dem beetles is fierce. Sure. Can't keep de cats off of eatin' dem, I can't. First t'ing you know dey've swallowed dem, and den dey gits thin and ties theirselves into knots.'

'You should put them into strait-waistcoats,' said Psmith. 'Passing, however, lightly – '

'Say, ever have a cross-eyed cat?'

'Comrade Jackson's cats,' said Psmith, 'have happily been almost free from strabismus.'

'Dey's lucky, cross-eyed cats is. You has a cross-eyed cat, and not'in' don't never go wrong. But, say, was dere ever a cat wit one blue eye and one yaller one in your bunch? Gum, it's fierce when it's like dat. It's a real skiddoo, is a cat wit one blue eye and one yaller one. Puts you in bad, surest t'ing you know. Oncest a guy give me a cat like dat, and first t'ing you know I'm in bad all round. It wasn't till I give him away to de cop on de corner and gets me one dat's cross-eyed dat I lifts de skiddoo off of me.'

'And what happened to the cop?' inquired Psmith, interested.

'Oh, he got in bad, sure enough,' said Mr Jarvis without emotion. 'One of de boys what he'd pinched and had sent to de Island once lays for him and puts one over him wit a black-jack. Sure. Dat's what comes of havin' a cat wit one blue eye and one yaller one.'

Mr Jarvis relapsed into silence. He seemed to be meditating on the inscrutable workings of Fate. Psmith took advantage of the pause to leave the cat topic and touch on matter of more vital import.

'Tense and exhilarating as is this discussion of the optical peculiarities of cats,' he said, 'there is another matter on which, if you will permit me, I should like to touch. I would hesitate to bore you with my own private troubles, but this is a matter which concerns Comrade Windsor as well as myself, and I know that your regard for Comrade Windsor is almost an obsession.'

'How's that?'

'I should say,' said Psmith, 'that Comrade Windso is a man to whom you give the glad hand.'

'Sure. He's to the good, Mr Windsor is. He caught me cat.'

'He did. By the way, was that the one that used to tie itself into knots?'

'Nope. Dat was anudder.'

'Ah! However, to resume. The fact is, Comrade Jarvis, we are much persecuted by scoundrels. How sad it is in this world! We look to every side. We look north, east, south, and west, and what do we see? Mainly scoundrels. I fancy you have heard a little about our troubles before this. In fact, I gather that the same scoundrels actually approached you with a view to en-gaging your services to do us in, but that you very handsomely refused the contract.'

'Sure,' said Mr Jarvis, dimly comprehending. 'A guy comes to me and says he wants you and Mr Windsor put through it, but I gives him de t'run down. "Nuttin' done," I says. "Mr Windsor caught me cat".'

'So I was informed,' said Psmith. 'Well, failing you, they went to a gentleman of the name of Reilly – '

'Spider Reilly?'

'You have hit it, Comrade Jarvis. Spider Reilly, the lessee and manager of the Three Points gang.'

'Dose T'ree Points, dey're to de bad. Dey're fresh.'

'It is too true, Comrade Jarvis.'

'Say,' went on Mr Jarvis, waxing wrathful at the recollection, 'what do youse t'ink dem fresh stiffs done de udder night. Started some rough woik in me own dance-joint.'

'Shamrock Hall?' said Psmith.

'Dat's right. Shamrock Hall. Got gay, dey did, with some of de Table Hillers. Say, I got it in for dem gazebos, sure I have. Surest t'ing you know.'

Psmith beamed approval.

'That,' he said, 'is the right spirit. Nothing could be more admirable. We are bound together by our common desire to check the ever-growing spirit of freshness among the members of the Three Points. Add to that the fact that we are united by a sympathetic knowledge of the manners and customs of cats, and especially that Comrade Jackson, England's greatest fancier, is our mutual friend, and what more do we want? Nothing.'

'Mr Jackson's to de good,' assented Mr Jarvis, eyeing Mike in friendly fashion.

'We are all to de good,' said Psmith. 'Now the thing I wished to ask you is this. The office of the paper on which I work was until this morning securely guarded by Comrade Brady, whose name will be familiar to you.'

'De Kid?'

'On the bull's-eye, as usual, Comrade Jarvis. Kid Brady, the coming light-weight champion of the world. Well, he has unfortunately been compelled to leave us, and the way into the office is consequently clear to any sand-bag specialist who cares to wander in. Matters connected with the paper have become so poignant during the last few days that an inrush of these same specialists is almost a certainty, unless – and this is where you come in.'

'Me?'

'Will you take Comrade Brady's place for a few days?'

'How's that?'

'Will you come in and sit in the office for the next day or so and help hold the fort? I may mention that there is money attached to the job. We will pay for your services. How do we go, Comrade Jarvis?'

Mr Jarvis reflected but a brief moment.

'Why, sure,' he said. 'Me fer dat. When do I start?'

'Excellent, Comrade Jarvis. Nothing could be better. I am obliged. I rather fancy that the gay band of Three Pointers who will undoubtedly visit the offices of *Cosy Moments* in the next few days, probably tomorrow, are due to run up against the surprise of their lives. Could you be there at ten tomorrow morning?'

'Sure t'ing. I'll bring me canister.'

'I should,' said Psmith. 'In certain circumstances one canister is worth a flood of rhetoric. Till tomorrow, then, Comrade Jarvis. I am very much obliged to you '

'Not at all a bad hour's work,' said Psmith complacently, as they turned out of Groome Street. 'A vote of thanks to you, Comrade Jackson, for your invaluable assistance.'

'It strikes me I didn't do much,' said Mike with a grin.

'Apparently, no. In reality, yes. Your manner was exactly right. Reserved, yet not haughty. Just what an eminent cat-fancier's manner should be. I could see that you made a pronounced hit with Comrade Jarvis. By the way, if you are going to show up at the office tomorrow, perhaps it would be as well if you were to look up a few facts bearing on the feline world. There is no knowing what thirst for information a night's rest may not give Comrade Jarvis. I do not presume to dictate, but if you were to make yourself a thorough master of the subject of catnip, for instance, it might quite possibly come in useful.'

25 Trapped

Mr Jarvis was as good as his word. On the following morning, at ten o'clock to the minute, he made his appearance at the office of *Cosy Moments,* his fore-lock more than usually well-oiled in honour of the occasion, and his right coat-pocket bulging in a manner that betrayed to the initiated eye the presence of the faithful 'canister'. With him, in addition to his revolver, he brought a long, thin young man who wore under his brown tweed coat a blue-and-red striped jersey. Whether he brought him as an ally in case of need or merely as a kindred soul with whom he might commune during his vigil, was not ascertained.

Pugsy, startled out of his wonted calm by the arrival of this distinguished company, observed the pair, as they passed through into the inner office, with protruding eyes, and sat speechless for a full five minutes. Psmith received the new-comers in the editorial sanctum with courteous warmth. Mr Jarvis introduced his colleague.

'Thought I'd bring him along. Long Otto's his monaker.'

'You did very rightly, Comrade Jarvis,' Psmith assured him. 'Your unerring instinct did not play you false when it told you that Comrade Otto would be as welcome as the flowers in May. With Comrade Otto I fancy we shall make a combination which will require a certain amount of tackling.'

Mr Jarvis confirmed this view. Long Otto, he affirmed, was no rube, but a scrapper from Biffville-on-the-Slosh. The hardiest hooligan would shrink from introducing rough-house proceedings into a room graced by the combined presence of Long Otto and himself.

'Then,' said Psmith, 'I can go about my professional duties with a light heart. I may possibly sing a bar or two. You will find cigars in that box. If you and Comrade Otto will select one apiece and group yourselves tastefully about the room in chairs, I will start in to hit up a slightly spicy editorial on the coming election.'

Mr Jarvis regarded the paraphernalia of literature on the table with interest. So did Long Otto, who, however, being a man of silent habit, made no comment. Throughout the *séance* and the events which followed it he confined himself to an occasional grunt. He seemed to lack other modes of expression. A charming chap, however.

'Is dis where youse writes up pieces fer de paper?' inquired Mr Jarvis, eyeing the table.

'It is,' said Psmith. 'In Comrade Windsor's pre-dungeon days he was wont to sit where I am sitting now, while I bivouacked over there at the smaller table. On busy mornings you could hear our brains buzzing in Madison Square Garden. But wait! A thought strikes me.' He called for Pugsy.

'Comrade Maloney,' he said, 'if the Editorial Staff of this paper were to give you a day off, could you employ it to profit?'

'Surest t'ing you know,' replied Pugsy with some fervour. 'I'd take me goil to de Bronx Zoo.'

'Your girl?' said Psmith inquiringly. 'I had heard no inkling of this, Comrade Maloney. I had always imagined you one of those strong, rugged, blood-and-iron men who were above the softer emotions. Who is she?'

'Aw, she's a kid,' said Pugsy. 'Her pa runs a delicatessen shop down our street. She ain't a bad mutt,' added the ardent swain. 'I'm her steady.'

'See that I have a card for the wedding, Comrade Maloney,' said Psmith, 'and in the meantime take her to the Bronx, as you suggest.'

'Won't youse be wantin' me today.'

'Not today. You need a holiday. Unflagging toil is sapping your physique. Go up and watch the animals, and remember me very kindly to the Peruvian Llama, whom friends have sometimes told me I resemble in appearance. And if two dollars would in any way add to the gaiety of the jaunt –'

'Sure t'ing. T'anks, boss.'

'It occurred to me,' said Psmith, when he had gone, 'that the probable first move of any enterprising Three Pointer who invaded this office would be to knock Comrade Maloney on the head to prevent his announcing him. Comrade Maloney's services are too valuable to allow him to be exposed to unnecessary perils. Any visitors who call must find their way in for themselves. And now to work. Work, the what's-its-name of the thingummy and the thing-um-a-bob of the what-d'you-call it.'

For about a quarter of an hour the only sound that broke the silence of the room was the scratching of Psmith's pen and the musical expectoration of Messrs Otto and Jarvis. Finally Psmith leaned back in his chair with a satisfied expression, and spoke.

'While, as of course you know, Comrade Jarvis,' he said, 'there is no agony like the agony of literary composition, such toil has its compensations. The editorial I have just completed contains its measure of balm. Comrade Otto will bear me out in my statement that there is a subtle joy in the manufacture of the well-formed phrase. Am I not right, Comrade Otto?'

The long one gazed appealingly at Mr Jarvis, who spoke for him.

'He's a bit shy on handin' out woids, is Otto,' he said.

Psmith nodded.

'I understand. I am a man of few words myself. All great men are like that. Von Moltke, Comrade Otto, and myself. But what are words? Action is the thing. That is the cry. Action. If that is Comrade Otto's forte, so much the better, for I fancy that action rather than words is what we may be needing in the space of about a quarter of a minute. At least, if the footsteps I hear without are, as I suspect, those of our friends of the Three Points.'

Jarvis and Long Otto turned towards the door. Psmith was right. Someone was moving stealthily in the outer office. Judging from the sound, more than one person.

'It is just as well,' said Psmith softly, 'that Comrade Maloney is not at his customary post. Now, in about a quarter of a minute, as I said – Aha!'

The handle of the door began to revolve slowly and quietly. The next moment three figures tumbled into the room. It was evident that they had not expected to find the door unlocked, and the absence of resistance when they applied their weight had had surprising effects. Two of the three did not pause in their career till they cannoned against the table. The third, who was holding the handle, was more fortunate.

Psmith rose with a kindly smile to welcome his guests.

'Why, surely!' he said in a pleased voice. 'I thought I knew the face. Comrade Repetto, this is a treat. Have you come bringing me a new hat?'

The white-haired leader's face, as he spoke, was within a few inches of his own. Psmith's observant eye noted that the bruise still lingered on the chin where Kid Brady's upper-cut had landed at their previous meeting.

'I cannot offer you all seats,' he went on, 'unless you care to dispose yourselves upon the tables. I wonder if you know my friend, Mr Bat Jarvis? And my friend, Mr L. Otto? Let us all get acquainted on this merry occasion.'

The three invaders had been aware of the presence of the great Bat and his colleague for some moments, and the meeting seemed to be causing them embarrassment. This may have been due to the fact that both Mr Jarvis and Mr Otto had produced and were toying meditatively with distinctly ugly-looking pistols.

Mr Jarvis spoke.

'Well,' he said, 'what's doin'?'

Mr Repetto, to whom the remark was directly addressed, appeared to have some difficulty in finding a reply. He shuffled his feet, and looked at the floor. His two companions seemed equally at a loss.

'Goin' to start any rough stuff?' inquired Mr Jarvis casually.

'The cigars are on the table,' said Psmith hospitably. 'Draw up your chairs, and let's all be jolly. I will open the proceedings with a song.'

In a rich baritone, with his eyeglass fixed the while on Mr Repetto, he proceeded to relieve himself of the first verse of 'I only know I love thee'.

'Chorus, please,' he added, as he finished. 'Come along, Comrade Repetto. Why this shrinking coyness? Fling out your chest, and cut loose.'

But Mr Repetto's eye was fastened on Mr Jarvis's revolver. The sight apparently had the effect of quenching his desire for song.

'"Lov' muh, ahnd ther world is – ah – mine!"' concluded Psmith.

He looked round the assembled company.

'Comrade Otto,' he observed, 'will now recite that pathetic little poem "Baby's Sock is now a Blue-bag". Pray, gentlemen, silence for Comrade Otto.'

He looked inquiringly at the long youth, who remained mute. Psmith clicked his tongue regretfully.

'Comrade Jarvis,' he said, 'I fear that as a smoking-concert this is not going to be a success. I understand, however. Comrade Repetto and his colleagues have come here on business, and nothing will make them forget it. Typical New York men of affairs, they close their minds to all influences that might lure them from their business. Let us get on, then. What did you wish to see me about, Comrade Repetto?'

Mr Repetto's reply was unintelligible.

Mr Jarvis made a suggestion.

'Youse had better beat it,' he said.

Long Otto grunted sympathy with this advice.

'And youse had better go back to Spider Reilly,' continued Mr Jarvis, 'and tell him that there's nothin' doin' in the way of rough house wit dis gent here.' He indicated Psmith, who bowed. 'And you can tell de Spider,' went on Bat with growing ferocity, 'dat next time he gits gay and starts in to shoot guys in me dance-joint I'll bite de head off'n him. See? Does dat go? If he t'inks his little two-by-four gang can put it across de Groome Street, he can try. Dat's right. An' don't fergit dis gent here and me is pals, and any one dat starts anyt'ing wit dis gent is going to have to git busy wit me. Does dat go?'

Psmith coughed, and shot his cuffs.

'I do not know,' he said, in the manner of a chairman addressing a meeting, 'that I have anything to add to the very well-expressed remarks of my friend, Comrade Jarvis. He has, in my opinion, covered the ground very thoroughly and satisfactorily. It now only remains for me to pass a vote of thanks to Comrade Jarvis and to declare this meeting at an end.'

'Beat it,' said Mr Jarvis, pointing to the door.

The delegation then withdrew.

'I am very much obliged,' said Psmith, 'for your courtly assistance, Comrade Jarvis. But for you I do not care to think with what a splash I might not have been immersed in the gumbo. Thank you, Comrade Jarvis. And you, Comrade Otto.'

'Aw chee!' said Mr Jarvis, handsomely dismissing the matter. Mr Otto kicked the leg of the table, and grunted.

For half an hour after the departure of the Three Pointers Psmith chatted amiably to his two assistants on matters of general interest. The exchange of ideas was somewhat one-sided, though Mr Jarvis had one or two striking items of information to impart, notably some hints on the treatment of fits in kittens.

At the end of this period the conversation was once more interrupted by the sound of movements in the outer office.

'If dat's dose stiffs come back – ' began Mr Jarvis, reaching for his revolver.

'Stay your hand, Comrade Jarvis,' said Psmith, as a sharp knock sounded on the door. 'I do not think it can be our late friends. Comrade Repetto's knowledge of the usages of polite society is too limited, I fancy, to prompt him to knock on doors. Come in.'

The door opened. It was not Mr Repetto or his colleagues, but another old friend. No other, in fact, than Mr Francis Parker, he who had come as an embassy from the man up top in the very beginning of affairs, and had departed, wrathful, mouthing declarations of war. As on his previous visit, he wore the dude suit, the shiny shoes, and the tall-shaped hat.

'Welcome, Comrade Parker,' said Psmith. 'It is too long since we met. Comrade Jarvis I think you know. If I am right, that is to say, in supposing that it was you who approached him at an earlier stage in the proceedings with a view to engaging his sympathetic aid in the great work of putting Comrade Windsor and myself out of business. The gentleman on your left is Comrade Otto.'

Mr Parker was looking at Bat in bewilderment. It was plain that he had not expected to find Psmith entertaining such company.

'Did you come purely for friendly chit-chat, Comrade Parker,' inquired Psmith, 'or was there, woven into the social motives of your call, a desire to talk business of any kind?'

'My business is private. I didn't expect a crowd.'

'Especially of ancient friends such as Comrade Jarvis. Well, well, you are breaking up a most interesting little symposium. Comrade Jarvis, I think I shall be forced to postpone our very entertaining discussion of fits in kittens till a more opportune moment. Meanwhile, as Comrade Parker wishes to talk over some private business – '

Bat Jarvis rose.

'I'll beat it,' he said.

'Reluctantly, I hope, Comrade Jarvis. As reluctantly as I hint that I would be alone. If I might drop in some time at your private residence?'

'Sure,' said Mr Jarvis warmly.

'Excellent. Well, for the present, good-bye. And many thanks for your invaluable cooperation.'

'Aw chee!' said Mr Jarvis.

'And now, Comrade Parker,' said Psmith, when the door had closed, 'let her rip. What can I do for you?'

'You seem to be all to the merry with Bat Jarvis,' observed Mr Parker.

'The phrase exactly expresses it, Comrade Parker. I am as a tortoiseshell kitten to him. But, touching your business?'

Mr Parker was silent for a moment.

'See here,' he said at last, 'aren't you going to be good? Say, what's the use of keeping on at this fool game? Why not quit it before you get hurt?'

Psmith smoothed his waistcoat reflectively.

'I may be wrong, Comrade Parker,' he said, 'but it seems to me that the chances of my getting hurt are not so great as you appear to imagine. The person who is in danger of getting hurt seems to me to be the gentleman whose name is on that paper which is now in my possession.'

'Where is it?' demanded Mr Parker quickly.

Psmith eyed him benevolently.

'If you will pardon the expression, Comrade Parker,' he said, ' "Aha!" Meaning that I propose to keep that information to myself.'

Mr Parker shrugged his shoulders.

'You know your own business, I guess.'

Psmith nodded.

'You are absolutely correct, Comrade Parker. I do. Now that *Cosy Moments* has our excellent friend Comrade Jarvis on its side, are you not to a certain extent among the Blenheim Oranges? I think so. I think so.'

As he spoke there was a rap at the door. A small boy entered. In his hand was a scrap of paper.

'Guy asks me give dis to gazebo named Smiff,' he said.

'There are many gazebos of that name, my lad. One of whom I am which, as Artemus Ward was wont to observe. Possibly the missive is for me.'

He took the paper. It was dated from an address on the East Side.

'Dear Smith,' it ran. 'Come here as quick as you can, and bring some money. Explain when I see you.'

It was signed 'W.W.'

So Billy Windsor had fulfilled his promise. He had escaped.

A feeling of regret for the futility of the thing was Psmith's first emotion. Billy could be of no possible help in the campaign at its present point. All the work that remained to be done could easily be carried through without his assistance. And by breaking out from the Island he had committed an offence which was bound to carry with it serious penalties. For the first time since his connexion with *Cosy Moments* began Psmith was really disturbed

He turned to Mr Parker.

'Comrade Parker,' he said, 'I regret to state that this office is now closing for the day. But for this, I should be delighted to sit cnatting with you. As it is – '

'Very well,' said Mr Parker. 'Then you mean to go on with this business?'

'Though it snows, Comrade Parker.'

They went out into the street, Psmith thoughtful and hardly realizing the other's presence. By the side of the pavement a few yards down the road a taximeter-cab was standing. Psmith hailed it.

Mr Parker was still beside him. It occurred to Psmith that it would not do to let him hear the address Billy Windsor had given in his note.

'Turn and go on down the street,' he said to the driver.

He had taken his seat and was closing the door, when it was snatched from his grasp and Mr Parker darted on to the seat opposite. The next moment the cab had started up the street instead of down, and the hard muzzle of a revolver was pressing against Psmith's waistcoat.

'Now what?' said Mr Parker smoothly, leaning back with the pistol resting easily on his knee.

26. A Friend in Need

'The point is well taken,' said Psmith thoughtfully.

'You think so?' said Mr Parker.

'I am convinced of it.'

'Good. But don't move. Put that hand back where it was.'

'You think of everything, Comrade Parker.'

He dropped his hand on to the seat, and remained silent for a few moments. The taxi-cab was buzzing along up Fifth Avenue now. Looking towards the window, Psmith saw that they were nearing the park. The great white mass of the Plaza Hotel showed up on the left.

'Did you ever stop at the Plaza, Comrade Parker?'

'No,' said Mr Parker shortly.

'Don't bite at me, Comrade Parker. Why be brusque on so joyous an occasion? Better men than us have stopped at the Plaza. Ah, the Park! How fresh the leaves, Comrade Parker, how green the herbage! Fling your eye at yonder grassy knoll.'

He raised his hand to point. Instantly the revolver was against his waistcoat, making an unwelcome crease in that immaculate garment.

'I told you to keep that hand where it was.'

'You did, Comrade Parker, you did. The fault,' said Psmith handsomely, 'was mine. Entirely mine. Carried away by my love of nature, I forgot. It shall not occur again.'

'It had better not,' said Mr Parker unpleasantly. 'If it does, I'll blow a hole through you.'

Psmith raised his eyebrows.

'That, Comrade Parker,' he said, 'is where you make your error. You would no more shoot me in the heart of the metropolis than, I trust, you would wear a made-up tie with evening dress. Your skin, however unhealthy to the eye of the casual observer, is doubtless precious to yourself, and you are not the man I take you for if you would risk it purely for the momentary pleasure of plugging me with a revolver. The cry goes round criminal circles in New York, "Comrade Parker is not such a fool as he looks." Think for a moment what would happen. The shot would ring out, and instantly bicycle-policemen would be pursuing this taxi-cab with the purposeful speed of greyhounds trying to win the Waterloo Cup. You would be headed off and stopped. Ha! What is this? Psmith, the People's Pet, weltering in his gore? Death to the assassin! I fear nothing could save you from the fury of the mob, Comrade Parker. I seem to see them meditatively plucking you limb from limb. "She loves me!" Off comes on arm. "She loves me not." A leg joins the little heap of limbs on the ground. That is how it would be. And what would you have left out of it? Merely, as I say, the momentary pleasure of potting me. And it isn't as if such a feat could give you the thrill of successful marksmanship. Anybody could hit a man with a pistol at an inch and a quarter. I fear you have not thought this matter out with sufficient care, Comrade Parker. You said to yourself, "Happy thought, I will kidnap Psmith!" and all your friends said, "Parker is the man with the big brain!" But now, while it is true that I can't get out, you are moaning, "What on earth shall I do with him, now that I have got him?" '

'You think so, do you?'

'I am convinced of it. Your face is contorted with the anguish of mental stress. Let this be a lesson to you, Comrade Parker, never to embark on any enterprise of which you do not see the end.'

'I guess I see the end of this all right.'

'You have the advantage of me then, Comrade Parker. It seems to me that we have nothing before us but to go on riding about New York till you feel that my society begins to pall.'

'You figure you're clever, I guess.'

'There are few brighter brains in this city, Comrade Parker. But why this sudden tribute?'

'You reckon you've thought it all out, eh?'

'There may be a flaw in my reasoning, but I confess I do not at the moment see where it lies. Have you detected one?'

'I guess so.'

'Ah! And what is it?'

'You seem to think New York's the only place on the map.'

'Meaning what, Comrade Parker?'

'It might be a fool trick to shoot you in the city as you say, but, you see, we aren't due to stay in the city. This cab is moving on.'

'Like John Brown's soul,' said Psmith, nodding. 'I see. Then you propose to make quite a little tour in this cab?'

'You've got it.'

'And when we are out in the open country, where there are no witnesses, things may begin to move?'

'That's it.'

'Then,' said Psmith heartily, 'till that moment arrives what we must do is to entertain each other with conversation. You can take no step of any sort for a full half-hour, possibly more, so let us give ourselves up to the merriment of the passing instant. Are you good at riddles, Comrade Parker? How much wood would a wood-chuck chuck, assuming for purposes of argument that it was in the power of a wood-chuck to chuck wood?'

Mr Parker did not attempt to solve this problem. He was sitting in the same attitude of watchfulness, the revolver resting on his knee. He seemed mistrustful of Psmith's right hand, which was hanging limply at his side. It was from this quarter that he seemed to expect attack. The cab was bowling easily up the broad street, past rows on rows of high houses, all looking exactly the same. Occasionally, to the right, through a break in the line of buildings, a glimpse of the river could be seen.

Psmith resumed the conversation.

'You are not interested in wood-chucks, Comrade Parker? Well, well, many people are not. A passion for the flora and fauna of our forests is innate rather than acquired. Let us talk of something else. Tell me about your home-life, Comrade Parker. Are you married? Are there any little Parkers running about the house? When you return from this very pleasant excursion will baby voices crow gleefully, "Fahzer's come home"?'

Mr Parker said nothing.

'I see,' said Psmith with ready sympathy. 'I understand. Say no more. You are unmarried. She wouldn't have you. Alas, Comrade Parker! However, thus it is! We look around us, and what do we see? A solid phalanx of the girls we have loved and lost. Tell me about her, Comrade Parker. Was it your face or your manners at which she drew the line?'

Mr Parker leaned forward with a scowl. Psmith did not move, but his right hand, as it hung, closed. Another moment and Mr Parker's chin would be in just the right position for a swift upper-cut . . .

This fact appeared suddenly to dawn on Mr Parker himself. He drew back quickly, and half raised the revolver. Psmith's hand resumed its normal attitude.

'Leaving more painful topics,' said Psmith, 'let us turn to another point. That note which the grubby stripling brought to me at the office purported to come from Comrade Windsor, and stated that he had escaped from Blackwell's Island, and was awaiting my arrival at some address in the Bowery. Would you mind telling me, purely to satisfy my curiosity, if that note was genuine? I have never made a close study of Comrade Windsor's handwriting, and in an unguarded moment I may have assumed too much.'

Mr Parker permitted himself a smile.

'I guess you aren't so clever after all,' he said. 'The note was a fake all right.'

'And you had this cab waiting for me on the chance?'

Mr Parker nodded.

'Sherlock Holmes was right,' said Psmith regretfully. 'You may remember that he advised Doctor Watson never to take the first cab, or the second. He should have gone further, and urged him not to take cabs at all. Walking is far healthier.'

'You'll find it so,' said Mr Parker.

Psmith eyed him curiously.

'What *are* you going to do with me, Comrade Parker?' he asked.

Mr Parker did not reply. Psmith's eye turned again to the window. They had covered much ground since last he had looked at the view. They were off Manhattan Island now, and the houses were beginning to thin out. Soon, travelling at their present rate, they must come into the open country. Psmith relapsed into silence. It was necessary for him to think. He had been talking in the hope of getting the other off his guard; but Mr Parker was evidently too keenly on the lookout. The hand that held the revolver never wavered. The muzzle, pointing in an upward direction, was aimed at Psmith's waist. There was no doubt that a move on his part would be fatal. If the pistol went off, it must hit him. If it had been pointed at his head in the orthodox way he might have risked a sudden blow to knock it aside, but in the present circumstances that would be useless. There was nothing to do but wait.

The cab moved swiftly on. Now they had reached the open country. An occasional wooden shack was passed, but that was all. At any moment the climax of the drama might be reached. Psmith's muscles stiffened for a spring. There was little chance of its being effective, but at least it would be better to put up some kind of a fight. And he had a faint hope that the suddenness of his movement might upset the other's aim. He was bound to be hit somewhere. That was certain. But quickness might save him to some extent.

He braced his leg against the back of the cab. In another moment he would have sprung; but just then the smooth speed of the cab changed to a series of jarring bumps, each more emphatic than the last. It slowed down, then came to a halt. One of the tyres had burst.

There was a thud, as the chauffeur jumped down. They heard him fumbling in the tool-box. Presently the body of the machine was raised slightly as he got to work with the jack.

It was about a minute later that somebody in the road outside spoke.

'Had a breakdown?' inquired the voice.

Psmith recognized it. It was the voice of Kid Brady.

27. Psmith Concludes His Ride

The Kid, as he had stated to Psmith at their last interview that he intended to do, had begun his training for his match with Eddie Wood, at White Plains, a village distant but a few miles from New York. It was his practice to open a course of training with a little gentle road-work; and it was while jogging along the highway a couple of miles from his training-camp, in company with the two thick-necked gentlemen who acted as his sparring-partners, that he had come upon the broken-down taxi-cab.

If this had happened after his training had begun in real earnest, he would have averted his eyes from the spectacle, however alluring, and continued on his way without a pause. But now, as he had not yet settled down to genuine hard work, he felt justified in turning aside and looking into the matter. The fact that the chauffeur, who seemed to be a taciturn man, lacking the conversational graces, manifestly objected to an audience, deterred him not at all. One cannot have everything in this world, and the Kid and his attendant thick-necks were content to watch the process of mending the tyre, without demanding the additional joy of sparkling small-talk from the man in charge of the operations.

'Guy's had a breakdown, sure,' said the first of the thick-necks.

'Surest thing you know,' agreed his colleague.

'Seems to me the tyre's punctured,' said the Kid.

All three concentrated their gaze on the machine.

'Kid's right,' said thick-neck number one. 'Guy's been an' bust a tyre.'

'Surest thing you know,' said thick-neck number two.

They observed the perspiring chauffeur in silence for a while.

'Wonder how he did that, now?' speculated the Kid.

'Guy ran over a nail, I guess,' said thick-neck number one.

'Surest thing you know,' said the other, who, while perhaps somewhat lacking in the matter of original thought, was a most useful fellow to have by one. A sort of Boswell.

'Did you run over a nail?' the Kid inquired of the chauffeur.

The chauffeur ignored the question.

'This is his busy day,' said the first thick-neck with satire. 'Guy's too full of work to talk to us.'

'Deaf, shouldn't wonder,' surmised the Kid. 'Say, wonder what he's doin' with a taxi so far out of the city.'

'Some guy tells him to drive him out here, I guess. Say, it'll cost him something, too. He'll have to strip off a few from his roll to pay for this.'

Psmith, in the interior of the cab, glanced at Mr Parker.

'You heard, Comrade Parker? He is right, I fancy. The bill –'

Mr Parker dug viciously at him with the revolver.

'Keep quiet,' he whispered, 'or you'll get hurt.'

Psmith suspended his remarks.

Outside, the conversation had begun again.

'Pretty rich guy inside,' said the Kid, following up his companion's train of thought. 'I'm goin' to rubber in at the window.'

Psmith, meeting Mr Parker's eye, smiled pleasantly. There was no answering smile on the other's face.

There came the sound of the Kid's feet grating on the road as he turned; and as he heard it Mr Parker, that eminent tactician, for the first time lost his head. With a vague idea of screening Psmith from the eyes of the man in the road he half rose. For an instant the muzzle of the pistol ceased to point at Psmith's waistcoat. It was the very chance Psmith had been waiting for. His left hand shot out, grasped the other's wrist, and gave it a sharp wrench. The revolver went off with a deafening report, the bullet passing through the back of the cab; then fell to the floor, as the fingers lost their hold. The next moment Psmith's right fist, darting upwards, took Mr Parker neatly under the angle of the jaw.

The effect was instantaneous. Psmith had risen from his seat as he delivered the blow, and it consequently got the full benefit of his weight, which was not small. Mr Parker literally crumpled up. His head jerked back, then fell limply on his chest. He would have slipped to the floor had not Psmith pushed him on to the seat.

The interested face of the Kid appeared at the window. Behind him could be seen portions of the faces of the two thick-necks.

'Ah, Comrade Brady!' said Psmith genially. 'I heard your voice, and was hoping you might look in for a chat.'

'What's doin', Mr Smith?' queried the excited Kid.

'Much, Comrade Brady, much. I will tell you all anon. Meanwhile, however, kindly knock that chauffeur down and sit on his head. He's a bad person.'

'De guy's beat it,' volunteered the first thick-neck.

'Surest thing you know,' said the other.

'What's been doin', Mr Smith?' asked the Kid.

'I'll tell you about it as we go, Comrade Brady,' said Psmith, stepping into the road. 'Riding in a taxi is pleasant provided it is not overdone. For the moment I have had sufficient. A bit of walking will do me good.'

'What are you going to do with this guy, Mr Smith?' asked the Kid, pointing to Parker, who had begun to stir slightly.

Psmith inspected the stricken one gravely.

'I have no use for him, Comrade Brady,' he said. 'Our ride together gave me as much of his society as I desire for today. Unless you or either of your friends are collecting Parkers, I propose that we leave him where he is. We may as well take the gun, however. In my opinion, Comrade Parker is not the proper man to have such a weapon. He is too prone to go firing it off in any direction at a moment's notice, causing inconvenience to all.' He groped on the floor of the cab for the revolver. 'Now, Comrade Brady,' he said, straightening himself up, 'I am at your disposal. Shall we be pushing off?'

It was late in the evening when Psmith returned to the metropolis, after a pleasant afternoon at the Brady training-camp. The Kid, having heard the details of the ride, offered once more to abandon his match with Eddie Wood, but Psmith would not hear of it. He was fairly satisfied that the opposition had fired their last shot, and that their next move would be to endeavour to come to terms. They could not hope to catch him off his guard a second time, and, as far as hired assault and battery were concerned, he was as safe in New York, now that Bat Jarvis had declared himself on his side, as he would have been in the middle of the desert. What Bat said was law on the East Side. No hooligan, however eager to make money, would dare to act against a protégé of the Groome Street leader.

The only flaw in Psmith's contentment was the absence of Billy Windsor. On this night of all nights the editorial staff of *Cosy Moments* should have been together to celebrate the successful outcome of their campaign. Psmith dined alone, his enjoyment of the rather special dinner which he felt justified in ordering in honour of the occasion somewhat diminished by the thought of Billy's hard case. He had seen Mr William Collier in *The Man from Mexico,* and that had given him an understanding of what a term of imprisonment on Blackwell's Island meant. Billy, during these lean days, must be supporting life on bread, bean soup, and water. Psmith, toying with the *hors d'oeuvre,* was somewhat saddened by the thought.

All was quiet at the office on the following day. Bat Jarvis, again accompanied by the faithful Otto, took up his position in the inner room, prepared to repel all invaders; but none arrived. No sounds broke the peace of the office except the whistling of Master Maloney.

Things were almost dull when the telephone bell rang. Psmith took down the receiver.

'Hullo?' he said.

'I'm Parker,' said a moody voice.

Psmith uttered a cry of welcome.

'Why, Comrade Parker, this is splendid! How goes it? Did

you get back all right yesterday? I was sorry to have to tear myself away, but I had other engagements. But why use the telephone? Why not come here in person? You know how welcome you are. Hire a taxi-cab and come right round.'

Mr Parker made no reply to the invitation.

'Mr Waring would like to see you.'

'Who, Comrade Parker?'

'Mr Stewart Waring.'

'The celebrated tenement house-owner?'

Silence from the other end of the wire.

'Well,' said Psmith, 'what step does he propose to take towards it?'

'He tells me to say that he will be in his office at twelve o'clock tomorrow morning. His office is in the Morton Building, Nassau Street.'

Psmith clicked his tongue regretfully.

'Then I do not see how we can meet,' he said. 'I shall be here.'

'He wishes to see you at his office.'

'I'm sorry, Comrade Parker. It is impossible. I am very busy just now, as you may know, preparing the next number, the one in which we publish the name of the owner of the Pleasant Street tenements. Otherwise, I should be delighted. Perhaps later, when the rush of work has diminished somewhat.'

'Am I to tell Mr Waring that you refuse?'

'If you are seeing him any time and feel at a loss for something to say, perhaps you might mention it. Is there anything else I can do for you, Comrade Parker?'

'See here – '

'Nothing? Then good-bye. Look in when you're this way.'

He hung up the receiver.

As he did so, he was aware of Master Maloney standing beside the table.

'Yes, Comrade Maloney?'

'Telegram,' said Pugsy. 'For Mr Windsor.'

Psmith ripped open the envelope.

The message ran:

'Returning today. Will be at office tomorrow morning,' and it was signed 'Wilberfloss'.

'See who's here!' said Psmith softly.

28. Standing Room Only

In the light of subsequent events it was perhaps the least bit unfortunate that Mr Jarvis should have seen fit to bring with him to the office of *Cosy Moments* on the following morning two of his celebrated squad of cats, and that Long Otto, who, as usual, accompanied him, should have been fired by his example to the extent of introducing a large and rather boisterous yellow dog. They were not to be blamed, of course. They could not know that before the morning was over space in the office would be at a premium. Still, it was unfortunate.

Mr Jarvis was slightly apologetic.

'T'ought I'd bring de kits along,' he said. 'Dey started in scrappin' yesterday when I was here, so today I says I'll keep my eye on dem.'

Psmith inspected the menagerie without resentment.

'Assuredly, Comrade Jarvis,' he said. 'They add a pleasantly cosy and domestic touch to the scene. The only possible criticism I can find to make has to do with their probable brawling with the dog.'

'Oh, dey won't scrap wit de dawg. Dey knows him.'

'But is he aware of that? He looks to me a somewhat impulsive animal. Well, well, the matter's in your hands. If you will undertake to look after the refereeing of any pogrom that may arise, I say no more.'

Mr Jarvis's statement as to the friendly relations between the animals proved to be correct. The dog made no attempt to annihilate the cats. After an inquisitive journey round the room he lay down and went to sleep, and an era of peace set in. The cats had settled themselves comfortably, one on each of Mr Jarvis's knees, and Long Otto, surveying the ceiling with his customary glassy stare, smoked a long cigar in silence. Bat breathed a tune, and scratched one of the cats under the ear. It was a soothing scene.

But it did not last. Ten minutes had barely elapsed when the yellow dog, sitting up with a start, uttered a whine. In the outer office could be heard a stir and movement. The next moment the door burst open and a little man dashed in. He had a peeled nose and showed other evidences of having been living in the open air. Behind him was a crowd of uncertain numbers. Psmith recognized the leaders of this crowd. They were the Reverend Edwin T. Philpotts and Mr B. Henderson Asher.

'Why, Comrade Asher,' he said, 'this is indeed a Moment of Mirth. I have been wondering for weeks where you could have got to. And Comrade Philpotts! Am I wrong in saying that this is the maddest, merriest day of all the glad New Year?'

The rest of the crowd had entered the room.

'Comrade Waterman, too!' cried Psmith. 'Why we have all met before. Except – '

He glanced inquiringly at the little man with the peeled nose.

'My name is Wilberfloss,' said the other with austerity. 'Will you be so good as to tell me where Mr Windsor is?'

A murmur of approval from his followers.

'In one moment,' said Psmith. 'First, however, let me introduce two important members of our staff. On your right, Mr Bat Jarvis. On your left, Mr Long Otto. Both of Groome Street.'

The two Bowery boys rose awkwardly. The cats fell in an avalanche to the floor. Long Otto, in his haste, trod on the dog, which began barking, a process which it kept up almost without a pause during the rest of the interview.

'Mr Wilberfloss,' said Psmith in an aside to Bat, 'is widely known as a cat fancier in Brooklyn circles.'

'Honest?' said Mr Jarvis. He tapped Mr Wilberfloss in friendly fashion on the chest. 'Say,' he asked, 'did youse ever have a cat with one blue and one yellow eye?'

Mr Wilberfloss side-stepped and turned once more to Psmith, who was offering B. Henderson Asher a cigarette.

'Who are you?' he demanded.

'Who am *I*?' repeated Psmith in an astonished tone.

'Who are you?'

'I am Psmith,' said the old Etonian reverently. 'There is a preliminary P before the name. This, however, is silent. Like the tomb. Compare such words as ptarmigan, psalm, and phthisis.'

'These gentlemen tell me you're acting sub-editor. Who appointed you?'

Psmith reflected.

'It is rather a nice point,' he said. 'It might be claimed that I appointed myself. Perhaps we may say, however, that Comrade Windsor appointed me.'

'Ah! And where is Mr Windsor?'

'In prison,' said Psmith sorrowfully.

'In prison!'

Psmith nodded.

'It is too true. Such is the generous impulsiveness of Comrade Windsor's nature that he hit a policeman, was promptly gathered in, and is now serving a sentence of thirty days on Blackwell's Island.'

Mr Wilberfloss looked at Mr Philpotts. Mr Asher looked at Mr Wilberfloss. Mr Waterman started, and stumbled over a cat.

'I never heard of such a thing,' said Mr Wilberfloss.

A faint, sad smile played across Psmith's face.

'Do you remember, Comrade Waterman – I fancy it was to you that I made the remark – my commenting at our previous interview on the rashness of confusing the unusual with the improbable? Here we see Comrade Wilberfloss, big-brained though he is, falling into the error.'

'I shall dismiss Mr Windsor immediately,' said the big-brained one.

'From Blackwell's Island?' said Psmith. 'I am sure you will earn his gratitude if you do. They live on bean soup there. Bean soup and bread, and not much of either.'

He broke off, to turn his attention to Mr Jarvis and Mr Waterman, between whom bad blood seemed to have arisen. Mr Jarvis, holding a cat in his arms, was glowering at Mr Waterman, who had backed away and seemed nervous.

'What is the trouble, Comrade Jarvis?'

'Dat guy dere wit two left feet,' said Bat querulously, 'goes and treads on de kit. I – '

'I assure you it was a pure accident. The animal – '

Mr Wilberfloss, eyeing Bat and the silent Otto with disgust, intervened.

'Who are these persons, Mr Smith?' he inquired.

'Poisson yourself,' rejoined Bat, justly incensed. 'Who's de little guy wit de peeled breezer, Mr Smith?'

Psmith waved his hands.

'Gentlemen, gentlemen,' he said, 'let us not descend to mere personalities. I thought I had introduced you. This, Comrade Jarvis, is Mr Wilberfloss, the editor of this journal. These, Comrade Wilberfloss – Zam-buk would put your nose right in a day – are, respectively, Bat Jarvis and Long Otto, our acting fighting-editors, vice Kid Brady, absent on unavoidable business.'

'Kid Brady!' shrilled Mr Wilberfloss. 'I insist that you give me a full explanation of this matter. I go away by my doctor's orders for ten weeks, leaving Mr Windsor to conduct the paper on certain well-defined lines. I return yesterday, and, getting into communication with Mr Philpotts, what do I find? Why, that in my absence the paper has been ruined.'

'Ruined?' said Psmith. 'On the contrary. Examine the returns, and you will see that the circulation has gone up every week. *Cosy Moments* was never so prosperous and flourishing. Comrade Otto, do you think you could use your personal influence with that dog to induce it to suspend its barking for a while? It is musical, but renders conversation difficult.'

Long Otto raised a massive boot and aimed it at the animal, which, dodging with a yelp, cannoned against the second cat and had its nose scratched. Piercing shrieks cleft the air.

'I demand an explanation,' roared Mr Wilberfloss above the din.

'I think, Comrade Otto,' said Psmith, 'it would make things a little easier if you removed that dog.'

He opened the door. The dog shot out. They could hear it being ejected from the outer office by Master Maloney. When there was silence, Psmith turned courteously to the editor.

'You were saying, Comrade Wilberfloss – ?'

'Who is this person Brady? With Mr Philpotts I have been going carefully over the numbers which have been issued since my departure – '

'An intellectual treat,' murmured Psmith.

and in each there is a picture of this young man in a costume which I will not particularize – '

'There is hardly enough of it to particularize.'

' – together with a page of disgusting autobiographical matter.'

Psmith held up his hand.

'I protest,' he said. 'We court criticism, but this is mere abuse. I appeal to these gentlemen to say whether this, for instance, is not bright and interesting.'

He picked up the current number of *Cosy Moments,* and turned to the Kid's page.

'This,' he said. 'Describing a certain ten-round unpleasantness with one Mexican Joe. "Joe comes up for the second round and he gives me a nasty look, but I thinks of my mother and swats him one in the lower ribs. He hollers foul, but nix on that. Referee says, 'Fight on.' Joe gives me another nasty look. 'All right, Kid,' he says; 'now I'll knock you up into the gallery.' And with that he cuts loose with a right swing, but I falls into the clinch, and then – !"'

'Bah!' exclaimed Mr Wilberfloss.

'Go on, boss,' urged Mr Jarvis approvingly. 'It's to de good, dat stuff.'

'There!' said Psmith triumphantly. 'You heard? Comrade Jarvis, one of the most firmly established critics east of Fifth Avenue, stamps Kid Brady's reminiscences with the hall mark of his approval.'

'I falls fer de Kid every time,' assented Mr Jarvis.

'Assuredly, Comrade Jarvis. You know a good thing when you see one. Why,' he went on warmly, 'there is stuff in these reminiscences which would stir the blood of a jelly-fish. Let me quote you another passage to show that they are not only enthralling, but helpful as well. Let me see, where is it? Ah, I have it. "A bully good way of putting a guy out of business is this. You don't want to use it in the ring, because by Queensberry Rules it's a foul; but you will find it mighty useful if any thick-neck comes up to you in the street and tries to start anything. It's this way. While he's setting himself for a punch, just place the tips of the fingers of your left hand on the right side of his chest. Then bring down the heel of your left hand. There isn't a guy living that could stand up against that. The fingers give you a leverage to beat the band. The guy doubles up, and you upper-cut him with your right, and out he goes." Now, I bet you never knew *that* before, Comrade Philpotts. Try it on your parishioners.'

'*Cosy Moments*,' said Mr Wilberfloss irately, 'is no medium for exploiting low prize-fighters.'

'Low prize-fighters! Comrade Wilberfloss, you have been misinformed. The Kid is as decent a little chap as you'd meet anywhere. You do not seem to appreciate the philanthropic motives of the paper in adopting Comrade Brady's cause. Think of it, Comrade Wilberfloss. There was that unfortunate stripling with only two pleasures in life, to love his mother and to knock the heads off other youths whose weight coincided with his own; and misfortune, until we took him up, had barred him almost completely from the second pastime. Our editorial heart was melted. We adopted Comrade Brady. And look at him now! Matched against Eddie Wood! And Comrade Waterman will support me in my statement that a victory over Eddie Wood means that he gets a legitimate claim to meet Jimmy Garvin for the championship.'

'It is abominable,' burst forth Mr Wilberfloss. 'It is disgraceful. I never heard of such a thing. The paper is ruined.'

'You keep reverting to that statement, Comrade Wilberfloss. Can nothing reassure you? The returns are excellent. Prosperity beams on us like a sun. The proprietor is more than satisfied.'

'The proprietor?' gasped Mr Wilberfloss. 'Does *he* know how you have treated the paper?'

'He is cognizant of our every move.'

'And he approves?'

'He more than approves.'

Mr Wilberfloss snorted.

'I don't believe it,' he said.

The assembled ex-contributors backed up this statement with a united murmur. B. Henderson Asher snorted satirically.

'They don't believe it,' sighed Psmith. 'Nevertheless, it is true.'

'It is not true,' thundered Mr Wilberfloss, hopping to avoid a perambulating cat. 'Nothing will convince me of it. Mr Benjamin White is not a maniac.'

'I trust not,' said Psmith. 'I sincerely trust not. I have every reason to believe in his complete sanity. What makes you fancy that there is even a possibility of his being – er – ?'

'Nobody but a lunatic would approve of seeing his paper ruined.'

'Again!' said Psmith. 'I fear that the notion that this journal is ruined has become an obsession with you, Comrade Wilberfloss. Once again I assure you that it is more than prosperous.'

'If,' said Mr Wilberfloss, 'you imagine that I intend to take your word in this matter, you are mistaken. I shall cable Mr White today, and inquire whether these alterations in the paper meet with his approval.'

'I shouldn't, Comrade Wilberfloss. Cables are expensive, and in these hard times a penny saved is a penny earned. Why worry Comrade White? He is so far away, so out of touch with our New York literary life. I think it is practically a certainty that he has not the slightest inkling of any changes in the paper.'

Mr Wilberfloss uttered a cry of triumph.

'I knew it,' he said, 'I knew it. I knew you would give up when it came to the point, and you were driven into a corner. Now, perhaps, you will admit that Mr White has given no sanction for the alterations in the paper?'

A puzzled look crept into Psmith's face.

'I think, Comrade Wilberfloss,' he said, 'we are talking at cross-purposes. You keep harping on Comrade White and his views and tastes. One would almost imagine that you fancied that Comrade White was the proprietor of this paper

Mr Wilberfloss stared. B. Henderson Asher stared. Every one stared, except Mr Jarvis, who, since the readings from the Kid's reminiscences had ceased, had lost interest in the discussion, and was now entertaining the cats with a ball of paper tied to a string.

'Fancied that Mr White . . . ?' repeated Mr Wilberfloss. 'I don't follow you. Who is, if he isn't?'

Psmith removed his monocle, polished it thoughtfully, and put it back in its place.

'I am,' he said.

29. The Knock-out for Mr Waring

'You!' cried Mr Wilberfloss.

'The same,' said Psmith.

'You!' exclaimed Messrs Waterman, Asher, and the Reverend Edwin Philpotts.

'On the spot!' said Psmith.

Mr Wilberfloss groped for a chair, and sat down.

'Am I going mad?' he demanded feebly.

'Not so, Comrade Wilberfloss,' said Psmith encouragingly. 'All is well. The cry goes round New York, "Comrade Wilberfloss is to the good. He does not gibber." '

'Do I understand you to say that you own this paper?'

'I do.'

'Since when?'

'Roughly speaking, about a month.'

Among his audience (still excepting Mr Jarvis, who was tickling one of the cats and whistling a plaintive melody) there was a tendency toward awkward silence. To start bally-ragging a seeming nonentity and then to discover he is the proprietor of the paper to which you wish to contribute is like kicking an apparently empty hat and finding your rich uncle inside it. Mr Wilberfloss in particular was disturbed. Editorships of the kind which he aspired to are not easy to get. If he were to be removed from *Cosy Moments* he would find it hard to place himself anywhere else. Editors, like manuscripts, are rejected from want of space.

'Very early in my connexion with this journal,' said Psmith. 'I saw that I was on to a good thing. I had long been convinced that about the nearest approach to the perfect job in this world, where good jobs are so hard to acquire, was to own a paper. All you had to do, once you had secured your paper, was to sit back and watch the other fellows work, and from time to time forward big cheques to the bank. Nothing could be more nicely attuned to the tastes of a Shropshire Psmith. The glimpses I was enabled to get of the workings of this little journal gave me the impression that Comrade White was not attached with any paternal fervour to *Cosy Moments*. He regarded it, I deduced, not so much as a life-work as in the light of an investment. I assumed that Comrade White had his price, and wrote to my father, who was visiting Carlsbad at the moment, to ascertain what that price might be. He cabled it to me. It was reasonable. Now it so happens that an uncle of mine some years ago left me a considerable number of simoleons, and though I shall not be legally entitled actually to close in on the opulence for a matter of nine months or so, I anticipated that my father would have no objection to staking me to the necessary amount on the security of my little bit of money. My father has spent some time of late hurling me at various professions, and we had agreed some time ago that the Law was to be my long suit. Paper-owning, however, may be combined with being Lord Chancellor, and I knew he would have no objection to my being a Napoleon of the Press on this side. So we closed with Comrade White, and – '

There was a knock at the door, and Master Maloney entered with a card.

'Guy's waiting outside,' he said.

'Mr Stewart Waring,' read Psmith. 'Comrade Maloney, do you know what Mahomet did when the mountain would not come to him?'

'Search me,' said the office-boy indifferently.

'He went to the mountain. It was a wise thing to do. As a general rule in life you can't beat it. Remember that, Comrade Maloney.'

'Sure,' said Pugsy. 'Shall I send the guy in?'

'Surest thing you know, Comrade Maloney.'

He turned to the assembled company.

'Gentlemen,' he said, 'you know how I hate to have to send you away, but would you mind withdrawing in good order? A somewhat delicate and private interview is in the offing.

Comrade Jarvis, we will meet anon. Your services to the paper have been greatly appreciated. If I might drop in some afternoon and inspect the remainder of your zoo – ?'

'Any time you're down Groome Street way. Glad.'

'I will make a point of it. Comrade Wilberfloss, would you mind remaining? As editor of this journal you should be present. If the rest of you would look in about this time tomorrow— Show Mr Waring in, Comrade Maloney.'

He took a seat.

'We are now, Comrade Wilberfloss,' he said, 'at a crisis in the affairs of this journal, but I fancy we shall win through.'

The door opened, and Pugsy announced Mr Waring.

The owner of the Pleasant Street tenements was of what is usually called commanding presence. He was tall and broad, and more than a little stout. His face was clean-shaven and curiously expressionless. Bushy eyebrows topped a pair of cold grey eyes. He walked into the room with the air of one who is not wont to apologize for existing. There are some men who seem to fill any room in which they may be. Mr Waring was one of these.

He set his hat down on the table without speaking. After which he looked at Mr Wilberfloss, who shrank a little beneath his gaze.

Psmith had risen to greet him.

'Won't you sit down?' he said.

'I prefer to stand.'

'Just as you wish. This is Liberty Hall.'

Mr Waring again glanced at Mr Wilberfloss.

'What I have to say is private,' he said.

'All is well,' said Psmith reassuringly. 'It is no stranger that you see before you, no mere irresponsible lounger who has butted in by chance. That is Comrade J. Fillken Wilberfloss, the editor of this journal.'

'The editor? I understood –'

'I know what you would say. You have Comrade Windsor in your mind. He was merely acting as editor while the chief was away hunting sand-eels in the jungles of Texas. In his absence Comrade Windsor and I did our best to keep the old journal

booming along, but it lacked the masterhand. But now all is
well: Comrade Wilberfloss is once more doing stunts at the old
stand. You may speak as freely before him as you would before
– well, let us say Comrade Parker.'

'Who are you, then, if this gentleman is the editor?'

'I am the proprietor.'

'I understood that a Mr White was the proprietor.'

'Not so,' said Psmith. 'There was a time when that was the
case, but not now. Things move so swiftly in New York
journalistic matters that a man may well be excused for not
keeping abreast of the times, especially one who, like yourself,
is interested in politics and house-ownership rather than in
literature. Are you sure you won't sit down?'

Mr Waring brought his hand down with a bang on the table,
causing Mr Wilberfloss to leap a clear two inches from his
chair.

'What are you doing it for?' he demanded explosively. 'I tell
you, you had better quit it. It isn't healthy.'

Psmith shook his head.

'You are merely stating in other – and, if I may say so,
inferior – words what Comrade Parker said to us. I did not
object to giving up valuable time to listen to Comrade Parker.
He is a fascinating conversationalist, and it was a privilege to
hob-nob with him. But if you are merely intending to cover the
ground covered by him, I fear I must remind you that this is
one of our busy days. Have you no new light to fling upon the
subject?'

Mr Waring wiped his forehead. He was playing a lost game,
and he was not the sort of man who plays lost games well. The
Waring type is dangerous when it is winning, but it is apt to
crumple up against strong defence.

His next words proved his demoralization.

'I'll sue you for libel,' said he.

Psmith looked at him admiringly.

'Say no more,' he said, 'for you will never beat that. For pure
richness and whimsical humour it stands alone. During the past
seven weeks you have been endeavouring in your cheery
fashion to blot the editorial staff of this paper off the face of the

earth in a variety of ingenious and entertaining ways; and now you propose to sue us for libel! I wish Comrade Windsor could have heard you say that. It would have hit him right.'

Mr Waring accepted the invitation he had refused before. He sat down.

'What are you going to do?' he said.

It was the white flag. The fight had gone out of him.

Psmith leaned back in his chair.

'I'll tell you,' he said. 'I've thought the whole thing out. The right plan would be to put the complete kybosh (if I may use the expression) on your chances of becoming an alderman. On the other hand, I have been studying the papers of late, and it seems to me that it doesn't much matter who gets elected. Of course the opposition papers may have allowed their zeal to run away with them, but even assuming that to be the case, the other candidates appear to be a pretty fair contingent of blighters. If I were a native of New York, perhaps I might take a more fervid interest in the matter, but as I am merely passing through your beautiful little city, it doesn't seem to me to make any very substantial difference who gets in. To be absolutely candid, my view of the thing is this. If the People are chumps enough to elect you, then they deserve you. I hope I don't hurt your feelings in any way. I am merely stating my own individual opinion.'

Mr Waring made no remark.

'The only thing that really interests me,' resumed Psmith, 'is the matter of these tenements. I shall shortly be leaving this country to resume the strangle-hold on Learning which I relinquished at the beginning of the Long Vacation. If I were to depart without bringing off improvements down Pleasant Street way, I shouldn't be able to enjoy my meals. The startled cry would go round Cambridge: "Something is the matter with Psmith. He is off his feed. He should try Blenkinsop's Balm for the Bilious." But no balm would do me any good. I should simply droop and fade slowly away like a neglected lily. And you wouldn't like *that,* Comrade Wilberfloss, would you?'

Mr Wilberfloss, thus suddenly pulled into the conversation, again leaped in his seat.

'What I propose to do,' continued Psmith, without waiting for an answer, 'is to touch you for the good round sum of five thousand and three dollars.'

Mr Waring half rose.

'Five thousand dollars!'

'Five thousand and three dollars,' said Psmith. 'It may possibly have escaped your memory, but a certain minion of yours, one J. Repetto, utterly ruined a practically new hat of mine. If you think that I can afford to come to New York and scatter hats about as if they were mere dross, you are making the culminating error of a misspent life. Three dollars are what I need for a new one. The balance of your cheque, the five thousand, I propose to apply to making those tenements fit for a tolerably fastidious pig to live in.'

'Five thousand!' cried Mr Waring. 'It's monstrous.'

'It isn't,' said Psmith. 'It's more or less of a minimum. I have made inquiries. So out with the good old cheque-book, and let's all be jolly.'

'I have no cheque-book with me.'

'I have,' said Psmith, producing one from a drawer. 'Cross out the name of my bank, substitute yours, and fate cannot touch us.'

Mr Waring hesitated for a moment, then capitulated. Psmith watched, as he wrote, with an indulgent and fatherly eye.

'Finished?' he said. 'Comrade Maloney.'

'Youse hollering fer me?' asked that youth, appearing at the door.

'Bet your life I am, Comrade Maloney. Have you ever seen an untamed mustang of the prairie?'

'Nope. But I've read about dem.'

'Well, run like one down to Wall Street with this cheque, and pay it in to my account at the International Bank.'

Pugsy disappeared.

'Cheques,' said Psmith, 'have been known to be stopped. Who knows but what on reflection, you might not have changed your mind?'

'What guarantee have I,' asked Mr Waring, 'that these attacks on me in your paper will stop?'

'If you like,' said Psmith, 'I will write you a note to that effect. But it will not be necessary. I propose, with Comrade Wilberfloss's assistance, to restore *Cosy Moments* to its old style. Some days ago the editor of Comrade Windsor's late daily paper called up on the telephone and asked to speak to him. I explained the painful circumstances, and, later, went round and hob-nobbed with the great man. A very pleasant fellow He asks to re-engage Comrade Windsor's services at a pretty size-able salary, so, as far as our prison expert is concerned, all may be said to be well. He has got where he wanted. *Cosy Moments* may therefore ease up a bit. If, at about the beginning of next month, you should hear a deafening squeal of joy ring through this city, it will be the infants of New York and their parents receiving the news that *Cosy Moments* stands where it did. May I count on your services, Comrade Wilberfloss? Excellent. I see I may. Then perhaps you would not mind passing the word round among Comrades Asher, Waterman, and the rest of the squad, and telling them to burnish their brains and be ready to wade in at a moment's notice. I fear you will have a pretty tough job roping in the old subscribers again, but it can be done. I look to you, Comrade Wilberfloss. Are you on?'

Mr Wilberfloss wriggling in his chair, intimated that he was.

30. Conclusion

It was a drizzly November evening. The streets of Cambridge were a compound of mud, mist, and melancholy. But in Psmith's rooms the fire burned brightly, the kettle droned, and all, as the proprietor had just observed, was joy, jollity, and song. Psmith, in pyjamas and a college blazer, was lying on the sofa. Mike, who had been playing football, was reclining in a comatose state in an arm-chair by the fire.

'How pleasant it would be,' said Psmith dreamily, 'if all our friends on the other side of the Atlantic could share this very peaceful moment with us! Or perhaps not quite all. Let us say, Comrade Windsor in the chair over there, Comrades Brady and Maloney on the table, and our old pal Wilberfloss sharing the floor with B. Henderson Asher, Bat Jarvis, and the cats. By the way, I think it would be a graceful act if you were to write to Comrade Jarvis from time to time telling him how your Angoras are getting on. He regards you as the World's Most Prominent Citizen. A line from you every now and then would sweeten the lad's existence.'

Mike stirred sleepily in his chair.

'What?' he said drowsily.

'Never mind, Comrade Jackson. Let us pass lightly on. I am filled with a strange content tonight. I may be wrong, but it seems to me that all is singularly to de good, as Comrade Maloney would put it. Advices from Comrade Windsor inform me that that prince of blighters, Waring, was rejected by an intelligent electorate. Those keen, clear-sighted citizens refused to vote for him to an extent that you could notice without a microscope. Still, he has one consolation. He owns what, when the improvements are completed, will be the finest and most commodious tenement houses in New York. Millionaires will stop

185

at them instead of going to the Plaza. Are you asleep, Comrade Jackson?'

'Um – m,' said Mike.

'That is excellent. You could not be better employed. Keep listening. Comrade Windsor also stated – as indeed did the sporting papers – that Comrade Brady put it all over friend Eddie Wood, administering the sleep-producer in the eighth round. My authorities are silent as to whether or not the lethal blow was a half-scissor hook, but I presume such to have been the case. The Kid is now definitely matched against Comrade Garvin for the championship, and the experts seem to think that he should win. He is a stout fellow, is Comrade Brady, and I hope he wins through. He will probably come to England later on. When he does, we must show him round. I don't think you ever met him, did you, Comrade Jackson?'

'Ur-r,' said Mike.

'Say no more,' said Psmith. 'I take you.'

He reached out for a cigarette.

'These,' he said, comfortably, 'are the moments in life to which we look back with that wistful pleasure. What of my boyhood at Eton? Do I remember with the keenest joy the brain-tourneys in the old form-room, and the bally rot which used to take place on the Fourth of June? No. Burned deeply into my memory is a certain hot bath I took after one of the foulest cross-country runs that ever occurred outside Dante's Inferno. So with the present moment. This peaceful scene, Comrade Jackson, will remain with me when I have forgotten that such a person as Comrade Repetto ever existed. These are the real Cosy Moments. And while on that subject you will be glad to hear that the little sheet is going strong. The man Wilberfloss is a marvel in his way. He appears to have gathered in the majority of the old subscribers again. Hopping mad but a brief while ago, they now eat out of his hand. You've really no notion what a feeling of quiet pride it gives you owning a paper. I try not to show it, but I seem to myself to be looking down on the world from some lofty peak. Yesterday night, when I was looking down from the peak without a cap and gown, a proctor slid up. Today I had to dig down into my jeans for a matter of two plunks. But what of it? Life must inevitably be dotted with these minor tragedies. I do not repine. The whisper goes round, "Psmith bites the bullet, and wears a brave smile." Comrade Jackson – '

A snore came from the chair.

Psmith sighed. But he did not repine. He bit the bullet. His eyes closed.

Five minutes later a slight snore came from the sofa, too. The man behind *Cosy Moments* slept.